This Stran...

'Do you remember your real name?'

'My what?'

Helker flipped over another page. 'Your father's real name is Casper Pelling.'

I would have laughed again if these guys hadn't seemed so convinced. That worried me. They seemed to have gone to a lot of trouble to make this stick.

I tried to be cold. 'My name is Patricia Meely.'

He smiled 'So have you always known the family secret?'

'What are you trying to trick me into?'

'The truth.'

'Which truth do you want?'

Robert Hawks was born in Indiana and still thinks of it as his home, though for several years he has been living in England with his wife and their two small daughters. He says that in writing *This Stranger, My Father*, he was trying to answer the question, What would happen if, tomorrow, you found out that everything you thought you knew about someone you loved was a lie. Would that make your love null and void? Would it matter at all? Do we ever really know each other?

PAN HORIZONS

C S Adler
Binding Ties

Judy Blume
Forever

Bruce Brooks
The Moves Make the Man

A E Cannon
Cal Cameron by Day, Spiderman by Night

Aiden Chambers
Dance on My Grave

Lois Duncan
The Eyes of Karen Connors
Stranger With My Face
I Know What You Did Last Summer

Paula Fox
The Moonlight Man

Anne Frank
The Diary of Anne Frank

Merril Joan Gerber
I'm Kissing as Fast as I Can
Also Known As Sadzia! The Belly Dancer

Virginia Hamilton
A Little Love

Toeckey Jones
Skindeep

M E Kerr
If I Love You Am I Trapped Forever?
Is that You, Miss Blue?
Night Kites
Son Of Someone Famous

Norma Klein
Beginner's Love
It's Not What You Expect
It's Okay If You Don't Love Me
Angel Face
Going Backwards
That's My Baby
No More Saturday Nights

Ron Koertge
Where the Kissing Never Stops

John MacLean
Mac

Harry Mazer
I Love You, Stupid

Richard Peck
Are You in the House Alone?
Remembering the Good Times
Close Enough To Touch

Sandra Scoppettone
Happy Endings Are All Alike

Jean Thesman
The Last April Dancers

Rosemary Wells
When No One Was Looking
The Man in the Woods

Barbara Wersba
Tunes for a Small Harmonica
Crazy Vanilla
Fat: A Love Story
Love Is the Crooked Thing
Beautiful Losers

Patricia Windsor
The Sandman's Eyes
The Hero

This Stranger, My Father

Robert Hawks

PAN HORIZONS

First published in the United States of America in 1988 by
Houghton Mifflin Company, Boston

First published in Great Britain in 1989 by
Pan Books Ltd, Cavaye Place, London SW10 9PG

9 8 7 6 5 4 3 2 1

© Robert E. Hawks II 1988

ISBN 0 330 30905 6

Printed and bound in Great Britain by
Richard Clay Ltd, Bungay, Suffolk

for
Sandra McCormick

ONE

Since I can't go back home anyway, this is what happened.

Before I was Karen Peterson I was Patricia Meely. Everyone called me Patty. I was somebody else even before that, but so very long ago that it's not like it was really me; it was just some kid who happened to grow up into me.

Honest, my life never used to be this confusing. I went to Karl Wallace Junior High School until this year when — finally — I got to start over at J. T. Kreuger Senior High School in Michigan City, which is where I lived. That's in Indiana, not Michigan. There has been some confusion over that one. Another thing is, up until that day — in the third month of my freshman year — I had only skipped three days of school ever: once to stand in line with Kimmers and her brother Ralph for concert tickets, and twice for the beach. Michigan City lies on the shore of

Lake Michigan, and I love the beach, the sunshine on my back (I never burn), and the sand in my toes (but not my hair!).

So it's not like I made it a habit to get into trouble or anything, unlike Kimmers, who was always drawing a line in the dirt and daring the world to cross it. She had even got herself into trouble earlier that day for calling her geography teacher, Mr. Ollosohn, a louse on the hide of mankind.

Kimmers had that magic way with words.

It was a real crummy day for July, but since it was November everything seemed perfect. The sky was bright and clear even though it was really cool outside. The clouds were high and fluffy white, just the way clouds are supposed to be. I'm fascinated with clouds. I like the way they slowly shapechange and move across the sky, keeping watch on the ground below as if they are shepherds put there to keep us all out of misery.

Good luck, guys.

I was watching the sky through the window of my algebra class and not the problems on the blackboard. Kimmers was sitting two rows behind me and to my left — an arrangement set up by Mrs. Zachs to keep us from whispering during class.

So we passed notes.

Despite what you may have heard, the real skill in good note-passing is not in the actual "hand-off." The passing of the note is a routine trick of the wrist which almost every second grader has mastered. The real skill is sitting in a deathly quiet algebra class and unfolding the note in such a way as to not make a lot of paper-crunching sounds that cause the teacher to look back and see you reading your lap.

The note was one word: *Well?*

I looked back at Kimmers. She jiggled her pencil at me.

Well?

I was tempted to write back *Well What?* just to drive her psychopathic, but I did want to answer her question, which was simply an abbreviated form of *Well did Mark Shiles ask you to the Homecoming dance after all and are you going to go with him or will you be going with Larry after all and if Mark did ask you what are you going to do with Larry you're not going to be stupid and tell Larry that you're sick are you?*

I thought about it.

I answered *I don't know.*

The details, I figured, could come later.

Details like how after a dozen feeble after-school phone calls Mark had finally gotten around to actually asking me out. I had been spinning my locker combination for about the third time and it finally snapped open when he asked me if I would go to the Homecoming dance with him. "Sure," I said. "Sounds like fun."

For a minute he looked almost sick. Green around

the gills, as Dad says. He asked a nervous question. "You don't think it'll be important for me to meet your parents first, do you?"

"What?" I slammed the locker shut.

"I mean I will if I have to, but parents don't seem to like me much." He scratched his chin. "I don't want to find out you suddenly couldn't go with me."

"So why couldn't I go?"

"Well, if your mom didn't like me or your dad thought I was too old or something . . ."

I shrugged. "First off, my mom is dead—"

Mark cringed. "Oh, God, I'm sorry—"

"—and second, my dad doesn't work like that."

"That's a relief," he said. Then he apologized again. "Listen, I'm sorry about your mom. I didn't know."

I shrugged again. "It was a long time ago. I hardly remember her."

He seemed to have a chill. "I don't know what I'd do if my mom . . ." His voice trailed off.

I was going to be late for class. "You get used to it," I said, which was not really true, I guess, because even though Dad and I had a really good thing going, I still had the dreams sometimes. Not always, but just often enough to bring me awake in the middle of the night, listening to the sounds of the house. Alone in my room in the dark, and more alone than that on the inside.

Algebra was our last class of the day and also the slowest hour. I wanted to do my special term project

in earth sciences on the time warps in math classes —
I wanted to use scientific method to prove that an
hour actually did stretch out over two or three when
you were confined in a small square room with a
middle-aged woman discussing axioms and variables.
Mr. Warner just laughed when I suggested it and
said that I should save the project for my special term
in sociology during my senior year. He claimed it was
more of a psychological problem than a scientific one,
but I'm not so sure.

It was five minutes until three, those bone-crushing
minutes that test the strongest wills. Mrs. Zachs always gave us the last fifteen minutes of class to get
started on our homework, but I never saw the point —
I could no more think in that classroom than I could
levitate. I was taking the opportunity to start the
letter to Larry, but it was not coming easy.

The *Dear Larry* was simple enough, but the first
line was a killer. I didn't want to hurt him any more
than I had to, but everything I thought of just came
across so badly.

This is hard for me to say . . .

Mrs. Zachs was looking at me then, but when she
saw the smirk of sheer disgust on my face she must
have assumed I was really doing my algebra for a
change, so she went back to her lesson plans. I reread
the line. I didn't know about Larry, but whenever I
got a note that started *This is hard for me to say*, I
immediately threw it away. Nothing good could
possibly follow.

How do you tell a guy that he is not a bad person, but that you have found somebody who you like much better?

I figured that I would have to wait and confer with Kimmers. Whenever it came to breaking off with a guy, Kimmers was the one to talk to. My only concern was that I wanted to sort of give Larry a break. I mean, I actually did like him; I just didn't like him any more than as a friend and I know how stupid that sounds. I wanted to let him down easy, not grind him up.

Grind him up. That was one of Kimmers' lines.

Class ended and I packed my stuff quickly. It was Friday and Dad was picking me up to take me over to Merrillville to the new shopping mall. Dad worked Swings and Mids at the Lacington Steel Mill, and Friday and Saturday were his days off, but Saturday afternoons he reserved for bowling. This was my only chance to get over to Merrillville before the Homecoming dance. Dad loved to bowl. He belonged to teams in two leagues and he still kept the scorecard from years before when he rolled a 280.

Kimmers pounced on me as soon as the bell stopped ringing, and I said yes, Mark had asked me, but now I had to figure out what to do about Larry. Kimmers immediately started being devious. She functioned well devious, and she followed me out into the hall, her mind clicking with all sorts of complicated plans to get around having to actually tell Larry that I was not going to the dance with him. "Why tell him at all?" she asked. "You never actually said that you were going with him, did you?"

I shook my head. "No. But so far this year we've gone to every dance together. I suspect he thinks we're going steady or something."

"Confused kid," said Kimmers.

Which was cruel, maybe, but Kimmers was always like that. Her real name is Kim Marz, but since the second grade everybody in the civilized world has called her Kimmers. She has been my best friend since then, even though she is not well liked at school.

Kimmers has one of the worst reputations around. Some girls I know wanted to vote Kimmers the girl most likely to commit mass murder — or to be murdered. That was mostly jealousy. I think what really annoys everybody most is that she always seems to be negative and sarcastic about everything and never seems to hold back an insult. She also has this crazed sense of social injustice, and whenever she feels that somebody has been wronged she goes off on one of her Kimmers Crusades. This plus her mouth got her suspended from Karl Wallace Junior High no less than four times for "instigation" and "subversion." Kimmers once tried to organize a boycott of the Wallace cafeteria when a student was refused lunch because he was two pennies short of the seventy-five-cent price. Kimmers started paying seventy-seven cents every day after that, which drove the cafeteria attendants crazy, and she circulated petitions for a boycott.

7

She was suspended from school, but her father called his lawyers, and two days later she was back, more angry at the world than ever.

That was back in junior high, and I have no doubt that the authorities wait in nervous anticipation of what she might do now that she is at Kreuger.

Nobody seems to understand the things about Kimmers that I do. This is the way she deals with today's world: She refuses to accept it on its own terms. She thinks the universe is a black comedy, and so she's developed an evil sense of humor to match it. Naturally because of all of this she is not a very popular personality at school, and she would really take a pounding there if it were not for one undeniable fact: She is beautiful. Not just pretty or attractive or whatever else you could mildly call some girls, but mind-bogglingly beautiful. Kimmers is years ahead of most of the girls in school in the figure department and she has the looks of a model: soft features, high cheekbones, blazing blue eyes, and her face is edged by blond hair which falls halfway down her back. I, on the other hand, look in the mirror each night before I go to bed and thank heaven above that guys like Mark don't see what I do: a plain, slightly freckled face with a nose too thin and sharp and too much curling hair which gets into my eyes.

I have to work constantly to keep myself presentable, but Kimmers seems to be able to just sit back and let it happen. Half of the guys in school are groaning themselves to sleep at night wanting to go out with her, but usually after a few times out she manages to drive them far away. If not, she simply dumps them. Hard. Because Kimmers has discovered the best possible way to avoid getting hurt in this world: View everything and everybody in it as a potential threat.

It's like the old story about the glass of water. The optimist will consider it half-full; the pessimist will consider it half-empty. Kimmers would consider it probably poisoned.

"Anyway," she was saying. "It's simple. Just go with Mark and if Larry shows up at your house that's his problem."

Even from Kimmers this shocked me. We were at my locker, stashing books. All except my algebra book, of course. Mrs. Zachs was the only teacher I ever had who assigned homework on Friday. Kimmers was already wearing her long gray jacket — her locker was way over on the other side of the school so she always got set to go home before she went to algebra.

I was shaking my head as I slammed the locker shut. "Just stand him up? I can't do that, it's so mean."

"Life is mean, Patty. Adjust to it."

"I can't be like you, Kimmers." Which was true; I could not be, even if I called a toll-free number on some quick-talking television ad and took a six-week correspondence course. I like to think of myself as being sensitive and easy-going, but Kimmers says I'm just a noodle and Dad says I'm naive. Whatever it is, I always seem to put myself in uncomfortable situations by trying to keep other people out of them. That's why I went to the first four dances with Larry.

The whole thing just kind of got out of control. He started calling me every night after dinner to talk about school and stuff, and once he came by on a Saturday afternoon for three hours and did nothing but watch me play records. I was terrified that one day he was going to break down and tell me he *loved* me. Then my life would really get complicated.

Kimmers shook her head as we headed for the front bus zone. "You can only paint yourself into so many corners," she said. Which was also true, but that didn't make it seem any less harsh.

"Do you want a ride home?" I asked, knowing of course that she would. Already students were crowding the loading zones, looking for their bus numbers and fussing with each other. Nobody in their right mind would choose a crowded bus of crazed students over a friendly car. "Avoid the bus," I said.

Kimmers grinned, holding up a cassette case. "We can play my tape." She had the new Walrus tape. Dad was always terrific about letting us play tapes instead of listening to his station on the radio, which was country and western of course.

I thought we might have to wait since Dad had said that morning that he might be late, but there he was, edging up with the other cars. Our car was a 1981 Mustang with a slight dent in the front fender on the driver's side. The car was light blue with no sign of rust. I was scheduled for driver's education second semester, which meant if I passed I could have my Indiana driver's license before my sophomore year. If I got a job during the summer and bought my own car, I would be able to drive myself and Kimmers to school.

I was thinking of asking Dad if maybe I could drive home for practice when I saw the first gray car screech around and cut Dad off.

Kimmers and I were standing on the walk, waiting for Dad to pull up, and we watched it all happen. There were three gray cars, all very slick and trim and professional-looking. They came in very fast and from different directions. The first gray sedan pulled around and cut Dad off so he couldn't pull our car forward, and a second gray sedan jammed in real tight so he couldn't back up. The third car screamed in over the sidewalk next to Dad and scattered the students who had been standing there waiting for their rides. I saw David and Ronnie Holt lose most of their books as they leaped clear of the racing car. The whole thing was fast and noisy, with squealing brakes and slamming doors as the men began to jump out of the sedans.

That was when I started to be frightened.

Everything else happening out in front of the school seemed to freeze just then. Nobody was joking or shoving. Nobody was getting into the school buses or the cars.

Everybody was watching.

The men in the gray cars wore three-piece suits with dark ties, and some had those black, wire-rimmed sunglasses that you see on pilots in the movies. They all had guns. A few were standing behind the gray car parked on the sidewalk, holding brown-handled shotguns, but most of them were waving pistols. Not those small .38s like the cops on television carry, but big, long-barreled pistols. They had Dad surrounded in the car and were yelling for him to come out . . . slowly.

I think I dropped my algebra book then.

Dad opened his door and started to rise up real slow. For just a second he looked at me, but I can't explain the expression on his face. It wasn't shame or surprise. I really couldn't tell what it was. He was trying to climb out of the car slow, but they didn't give him a chance. Two of the graysuits stepped forward, pulled him out by the shoulders, and slammed him against the hood. They stuck their pistols in the back of his neck.

I knew, right then, that they were going to shoot him.

I tried to scream but no sound came out.

They did not shoot him, though; they just kicked his legs wide apart and started searching him. When they were satisfied with that, they handcuffed him.

There was almost no sound.

Dad was lying there, his face pressed tight against the hood while they put handcuffs on him, but the men in the gray suits would not lower their guns.

Two of them seemed to be saying something to Dad, but the noise and buzz of excitement had resumed, and I couldn't hear.

Then another graysuit appeared. A weasel-faced man with a thin wire mustache walked over to me and Kimmers. He was carrying a black walkie-talkie radio. Suddenly he reached out and grabbed me by the arm. "Patricia Meely, come with me please."

I tugged back against his pull and Kimmers turned on him and exploded: "Hey, what do you think you're doing!" A second graysuit got between Kimmers and me and took my other arm. Kimmers slugged him hard in the small of the back. "That's my friend!" she yelled.

The two graysuits ignored Kimmers, and the one with the radio muttered into it as they walked me quickly to the sedan on the sidewalk. Dad was nowhere to be seen — they had obviously put him into one of the other cars. The two graysuits who had handcuffed Dad stepped aside to let the other two lead me to the car. I never really fought back, but when I tried to slow down a bit they lifted me gently by the elbows and almost carried me. The guy with the walkie-talkie opened the back door of the car and crawled in, tugging me in behind him. The second graysuit followed me in and locked his door.

The car stank of pipe smoke and that cheap stuff that people use to try to make the upholstery of old cars seem new. The two guys who had arrested Dad locked their shotguns in the trunk and climbed in up front. The driver started the engine while the other man mumbled something into his radio.

The guy with the walkie-talkie asked the guys up front, "Does she need Miranda?"

The driver put the car in gear and nodded. "Just in case."

Old graysuit put his walkie-talkie into a case built into his door and pulled a card from his jacket pocket. He started reading it, and it was just like it always is in all of those boring cop shows on television. The car was moving up through the crowds of kids trying to look in at me, and I saw Kimmers standing, confused, by the stone lion which guarded the front of our school, and the guy reading did not care at all. He just blandly read on.

"Patricia Meely, you have the right to remain silent, that is to say nothing at all. You have the right to an attorney. . . ." He kept reading as they pulled away from the school, but after a while I stopped hearing anything.

TWO

I figured they were taking me to jail, but I was wrong.

They drove me out of the city, and all the while I was trying to figure out what I had done. Why had they arrested Dad? For the longest time they wouldn't even tell me where they were taking me, but finally the graysuit who had read me my rights said simply, "The Federal Building."

"Where is that?" I asked.

He shrugged. "South Bend."

South Bend is the St. Joseph County seat. It's about an hour and fifteen minutes' drive east from Michigan City.

I was scared, and whenever I'm nervous I tend to babble. Without even meaning to, I started talking to the graysuits. "Any of you guys have names?" I asked.

The graysuit who had answered me shrugged again. "I'm Agent Walkins, this is Agent Munroe."

I looked over. The graysuit sitting on the other side of me nodded. Agent Munroe.

"What about first names?"

Walkins looked over at me and sneered. *"Agent."*

I nodded. "Agent. Like CIA agents?"

"FBI."

"Ah." I nodded again. Right. "Is my dad going to be in South Bend?" No answer. "Is there any particular reason that you guys are taking me there?"

Nobody would say.

When we arrived in South Bend the driver drove right under a huge, new glass building and into one of those dark underground parking garages. He found his parking space and then Walkins and Munroe took me out of the car, led me to an elevator, and brought me to the fourth floor. When the elevator doors opened, the brightness almost knocked me down.

Everything on the floor seemed to be white: the highly polished floors, the walls, the ceiling, the lights. White with this infestation of graysuits. There were even a few gray-suited women — they wore gray skirts instead of trousers. I was led to an office with a door marked INTERROGATION TWO. Walkins gestured me inside. "You'll wait here," he said.

"Whatever," I replied.

I went inside alone and they pulled the door shut behind me. The room was bare except for two chairs and a table in between. There was a thick red book lying on the table: a dictionary. There was no window.

They had taken my purse, and my algebra book was last seen lying in front of the school, so there wasn't much to do in the room while I waited but worry about Dad and wonder what it was they were doing to him. I tried out both chairs and decided that neither one was very comfortable. I looked up some words in the dictionary.

Dissimilitude: Noun. Lack of resemblance.

Happenstance: Noun. A chance occurrence or accident.

Supercilious: Adjective. Characterized by haughty scorn; disdainful.

Zephyr: Noun. The west wind.

The door snapped open and two men came in.

One was another typical graysuit with a waxy-looking face and a receding hairline. His mouth twitched when he smiled. He carried an expensive-looking black briefcase. I started to get up when they came in, but he just gestured back and said, "Sit, please." The second man was out of the ordinary, wearing a brown jacket and tie and not looking very happy in either. He carried a small cassette tape player and a shoebox. He set the tape player flat on the table about a foot in front of me and turned it on; then he crossed his arms and stepped back quietly against the door.

Just an observer, I thought.

The graysuit sat across from me and pulled some papers from his briefcase before putting it on the floor at his feet. "Patricia," he said. "My name is Robert Helker. I am a special agent for the FBI. Do you know what that is?"

I nodded. "Federal Bureau of Investigation."

He smiled and twitched and nodded. "Exactly. This gentleman is Walter Rogers of the United States Marshals Service. We will be recording this interview."

"Why am I here?"

Helker pulled a pen from his pocket and began flipping through the papers he had placed on the table before him. He opened up a small notebook. "Right now all we want to do is ask you some questions," he said.

"Where is my dad?"

"He's in custody."

"Why?"

"Why don't you tell me?" Helker smiled again.

"I don't know," I said.

"What do you know?"

I frowned. "You guys are weird."

Helker laughed and turned over a paper. "Patricia, do you know that your father's real name is not Douglas Meely?"

"What?"

"Do you know who your father really is?"

"What do you mean, do I know who he really is?" I was beginning to really worry now. These guys were obviously lost. I had read about times when the police raided the wrong apartment or sent a man to prison for a crime he never committed. "Where did you guys take him?"

"Patricia, what did your father do for a living?"

"He works at the mill."

"Did he make a lot of money there?"

"Enough," I said. Then my blood froze. "What do you mean *did* for a living?"

Helker smiled really wide now and the twitch was driving me crazy. "So," he said. "Have you always known about your father?"

"What?"

"Was it treated like the family secret?"

"What secret?" I didn't know what this guy Helker was looking for, but I was positive he had the wrong guy and the wrong guy's daughter.

"It's all right to talk about it, Patricia," he said. "We know most of it now, anyway. It's over. It would help if you talk about it with us."

"Talk about what?" I asked. "I don't know what you loons are talking about."

"Patty . . ." It was Rogers, the U.S. marshal. His voice was thick and deep like a grandfather's. "Did you know that your father is an escapee from a federal penitentiary?"

Now I laughed, relieved. They *did* have the wrong guy. I had been terrified, up until that point, that the government had found out about Dad cheating on his income taxes. I knew that Dad sometimes worked

19

for Mr. Laskey on weekends at his garage and was paid in cash. Dad said everybody did it, and I figured that was probably true. I had been scared that he had finally been caught, but this prison thing was actually funny, so I laughed, the air rushing out of me. "Guys," I said. "I'm afraid you snatched the wrong person."

Helker smiled. "Why is that?"

"We've been living in Michigan City for fifteen years."

Helker shook his head. "Nope. Moved there about twelve years ago. From Pennsylvania, it seems."

"Pennsylvania? That's wrong — Mom's family are all from Ohio."

Helker continued to shake his head slowly.

I shrugged. "I was young when we moved. I don't remember."

"Do you remember your real name?"

"My what?"

Helker flipped over another paper. "Your father's real name is Casper Pelling."

I would have laughed again if these guys hadn't seemed so convinced. That worried me. They seemed to have gone to a lot of trouble to make this stick. "Casper what?"

"Casper Pelling. So at the very least that makes you Patricia Pelling. It's fairly obvious that Casper used a variety of aliases after his escape. It may take some time to determine which one he was using when you were born. Actually, it's irrelevant. You'll still be a Pelling, but we might discover that your first name isn't really Patty. We're checking into all that."

I tried to be cold. "My name is Patricia Meely."

He smiled. "So have you always known the family secret?"

"What are you trying to trick me into?"

"The truth."

"Which truth do you want?"

Helker frowned. "Oh, there is only one truth, Patricia Pelling —"

I yelled, "My name is Meely!"

He yelled back. "Your name is whatever I say it is!"

I jumped. Rogers looked over sharply, but Helker didn't even twitch this time when he smiled. Calmer now. "We're going to get to the truth at some point this evening. I have nowhere else to go. And neither, I suspect, do you."

"What is going on here?" I asked.

"We just don't think it possible for a man to keep something like this from his family for so many years."

"I don't know what you're talking about," I said. "My dad was never in prison so he couldn't very well escape from it."

"Your father thought we gave up, Patricia." Helker shook his head. "We don't give up. We never give up."

I frowned. "You're very supercilious."

He looked up from his pad. "What is that supposed to mean?"

"Look it up in your dictionary."

Helker pulled a brown file folder from his briefcase

and set it before him on the table. "Did you know that your dad was a traitor?"

"A what?"

"I've got a few interesting things for you to read, Patricia." He started flipping through the contents of the file: it was full of photographs and photocopies of old magazine and newspaper articles. He smiled without the twitch again and passed the file across to me. I didn't try to read any more than just the headlines, but I did look at the photographs.

In almost every one of them, looking years younger and maybe a little dazed, was my dad.

The caption underneath one of them read, "Casper Pelling being removed from the Baker County Jail following indictment on thirty-three counts of espionage."

The newspapers all said that my dad was a spy.

The headlines were pretty consistent and very vicious. All about some "Pelling-Schmeer" conspiracy to sell top-secret stuff to the Soviet Union.

Helker spoke while I read. "Your father and a man named Alan Schmeer worked for JTR Electronics back in 1964. They weren't making bad money for the time, but they decided to finance a few extras by peddling some electronic data systems to the Soviets. The Russians used this stuff to make nuclear missiles, which are even now aimed at us here in this room. Your dad was a swell guy. He sold out his country for money."

Helker scratched something on the pad and

chuckled. "Eventually, of course, they got caught. Alan Schmeer took the easy way out. He got wind that your father had been arrested, so he climbed into a warm bath and opened up both of his wrists. That might have worked out best for your dad, but it turned out Alan Schmeer kept a diary that told the whole story. It was entered as evidence, and Casper Pelling got slammed: fifty years in a maximum-security prison."

Helker sighed and looked up. "That left only one more question. In the diary Alan Schmeer mentioned the last payoff just before your dad got arrested. It was supposed to have been almost a hundred thousand dollars. Casper was to collect it and they would split it later. Only later never came." Helker frowned across the table at me. "Casper Pelling claimed the money did not exist. Everyone thought he was a fool for not giving it up to chop his sentence down a few years, but Casper fooled everyone. He escaped from prison in 1966. He was on the lam for almost twenty years. That ended today."

Helker stared at me another minute, as if he were expecting me to say something, but then he switched off the tape recorder and started stuffing his papers back into his briefcase. He left me the file folder full of clippings. "You go ahead and read those clippings. Find out what sort of man your father really is. We'll be talking to you later."

Marshal Rogers took the tape out of the recorder and put it into the shoebox. Then he took the box and the recorder and followed Helker out into the hall.

Alone with the file and the dictionary, I tried to come to grips with what was happening. It was a big lie, obviously. Evil and ugly. It was like one of those nightmare Hitchcock movies, where an innocent man is chased across the country for a murder he did not commit. Absolutely no one believes that he is innocent, not even the police. I remembered reading tales of innocent people spending ten and twenty years in prison because of mistaken identities. Now I was terrified; this was not happening on TV or in the movies. It was happening to my dad.

I sat down in Helker's chair and carefully arranged the clippings from the folder, placing them in order by date. I had to find something that might help. I knew for this one we would need more than just lawyers: The government, or whoever it was behind all of this, had fixed things up well.

I read everything in the file once. I read everything in it twice. One article I read almost five times, concentrating on every paragraph, every sentence, every word, until my eyes started to ache and my head throbbed. It was a long magazine piece, obviously written much later than the others. It was one of those profiles that try to get inside the heads of those involved and claim to tell you what they were thinking about when the events unfolded. It attempted to "recreate" the events as they happened.

The article was called "The Sandman and Killjoy,"

and by the time I closed the file folder I felt hollow, as if worms had eaten away my insides. I left the clippings on the table and sat myself in a corner of the room, my back against the wall. I tried to imagine a reason for all of this.

It was 1962, said the article. John F. Kennedy was president of the United States, haircuts were short, and the Beatles were just another English group trying to make the big time. Missiles were new as well. The first Minutemen were being constructed in Montana and the Dakotas, and the Russians had nothing to compare with them. President Kennedy had called the Minuteman his "ace in the hole" during the Cuban missile crisis. Security was tight around the entire project until a hazel-eyed man who was missing the pinkie finger of his left hand walked into the Soviet Embassy in Mexico City and offered to give the entire project to them on a platter — for a price.

That man was Alan Schmeer, who was known as Killjoy to his coworkers at JTR Electronics. Killjoy had few friends and was very alienated. He was constantly teased at work, and no one teased harder than a fair-haired young man with a wide smile and a dream of sailing a sloop around the world. The young man's name was Casper Pelling. Everyone called him the Sandman because of the sleepy way he carried himself around in the mornings after long nights. "Even looking at you makes me tired," they would remark.

Sitting now in the corner of the office, shivering

even though it was warm, I thought about Dad and his heavy eyelids. And his talk about the boat he wanted to buy some day.

The article was full of small details that were bringing the wetness to my eyes and the rock to my throat. Casper Pelling loved to bowl. He was on the shop team at JTR. The Sandman loved chocolate. The Sandman worked part-time as an automobile mechanic.

I'm not sure, but I think that was when I finally started to cry.

Black Pigeon and Cold Pigeon were the code names the KGB gave to the operatives who finally managed to crack the security around the Minuteman missile program. But the men and women who worked with Black and Cold Pigeon knew them as the Sandman and Killjoy.

I cried until I lost track of time and then I cried just a little while longer. I was in shock, I guess. I was not crying so much over what my dad had supposedly done; I was crying out of the loneliness of being forced to confront it all by myself. I was locked in a room of the Federal Building in South Bend, by myself, and that slime Helker had just ended my life with a folder of twenty-year-old clippings.

When I could not cry anymore, I waited.

The door finally opened and a man wearing a tan suit came in. He was tall and dark, with a half beard and patchy spots where the rest was trying to grow in, and he tugged at the tie he wore. "End of the day," he explained. "Sorry." He loosened the tie and set his briefcase on the table. "You look tired," he said, nodding to me. "Are you all right?"

"I want to talk to Helker."

"I think they're finished with you for tonight. They said I could take you."

"I need to talk to him."

"I'm sure they'll see you tomorrow."

"Who are you?"

"Greg Raintree," he said. "Social services. Why don't you come over here and sit down for a minute?"

I shrugged and got up from my corner. I knew that my face was probably red and puffy, but I no longer cared. They had taken my purse with my make-up, so there was nothing I could do about it. Raintree had a front tooth that was half-broken, so I mentioned it. "Been eating plaster apples?"

He smiled, and it looked almost genuine. "I got popped in the face with a softball this summer. It doesn't hurt, but sometimes I whistle when I talk. I'm still waiting to get it capped." He pulled a small booklet from his briefcase and passed it across to me. "Why don't you read through this —"

I started to object that I had done more than enough reading for one day when I saw the title of the booklet: *Living with Foster Families*.

"Oh, come on now, no way —" I started.

"I'm sorry about this, Patty, but you're a ward of the state of Indiana now."

"Can't I stay with friends, then?"

"That would be difficult, if not impossible," he said. "There is going to be a lot of publicity on this. In fact, it has already started. Some new factors are starting to come to light. . . ."

"Are you saying that my friends might not like me anymore? That's crazy."

"People are only human, Patty. Sometimes they don't react as you feel they should."

"Let me call Kimmers. Her mom lets me spend the night all the time."

"This amounts to quite a bit more than just spending the night somewhere, Patty. I'm sorry. Actually, it's lucky they got in touch with me before I left the office tonight. I don't usually wear my beeper on Friday nights. I was on my way out the door. You might very well have spent the night in the lockup."

"In the what?"

"The juvenile lockup." He explained what that meant. Jail for kids under eighteen years of age.

"But I didn't do anything."

"That's not really the point," he said. "There wouldn't have been anywhere else to place you. But we're good to go now. Just as soon as I get some information down."

He copied my birthday, full name, and the fact that I was female with no immediate medical problems. I asked him what they had done with my dad, but he ignored the question. "Okay," I said. "What are you guys doing with me?"

"Well, I'm just with social services," he said. "It's

my understanding that you're not being charged with anything, but the way things stand now, you will not be going back to Michigan City."

"What? You mean never?"

"I can't say."

"So where am I going?"

"We're going to set you up in a local foster home until we can unscramble all of the running your father did. It will take us a while to determine who your nearest relative is."

I nodded. "What you mean is that it will take you a while to figure out who wants me."

"Sometimes it works out that way."

"My dad always said that most of our relatives were lowlifes. That was why we never saw any of them."

Raintree frowned. "He may have had other reasons. You might be pleasantly surprised."

I asked if the foster family would be coming down to pick me up, and he answered that it was possible but not required. He would probably drive me over to their house.

"What happens if I don't want to stay?"

"You will be listed as a runaway."

"I wouldn't be a runaway," I said. "I'd just go home. We have a house. A car. Lots of food."

"Those are all in dispute."

"They belong to us."

"The IRS has a claim."

"What?"

"Misrepresentation of federal tax returns."

"You just can't take our lives away like this."

Raintree shrugged. He finished scribbling the last bit of personal data on his form. "It was my understanding that it was not your father's life to live. He owed fifty years."

"This is wrong."

"Patty, there are no charges against you right now. But if you run away before we can locate a relative, you will be a runaway ward of the state. That is an offense. You could wind up in a reform school. You certainly don't want that."

"I am not a piece of property," I said. "I don't need to be claimed like a scarf in a lost-and-found box."

"I'm sorry," he said. From the way he sounded, he was either very tired or really sorry.

THREE

The only thing tolerable about the Gizzales' house was their cat. They called him Mr. Wise. He was an old tabby, lumpy and gray with fading black stripes up and down his back. Neither of the Gizzales ever spoke to him or cuddled him, or petted him. The most attention I ever saw them show Mr. Wise was to fill his bowl with generic cat food or shove open the back door to let him in or out of the house.

He was a slow mover, that cat. Sometimes he would be collapsed in a corner, like a pile of dirty shirts, and you would have to move in real close to see if he was even breathing. He always was, though, and would open his eyes slowly and sort of cock his head back, as if to say, "Yes, may I help you?"

Mr. Wise, like the best of cats, had personality.

Mr. Gizzale, like the worst of people, had little.

Raintree had driven me across town to the Gizzales' house after all the forms had been completed to his satisfaction. On the way over he talked about himself, out of guilt mostly, I suppose. He told me that he was half Cherokee Indian on his father's side, and he hoped to get his Ph.D. in psychology some day. He didn't ask me anything about myself.

The Gizzales lived on a side of South Bend that I had never seen before. It was not exactly falling apart, but everything over there seemed to have a nervous, propped-up feeling about it, as if one false move would bring the entire neighborhood crashing down into a pile of bricks and splintered wood. The house was a musky-smelling red brick place which seemed to serve no purpose other than to secure the lawn against neighborhood kids on bicycles. Mr. Gizzale's favorite pastime seemed to be leaping from his chair and tossing open the front door in order to shout at some ten-year-old who took a short cut across the yard.

Mrs. Gizzale was a coupon collector. She kept little brown file boxes stuffed with clippings from newspapers or the hundreds of old magazines she had stacked in almost every room of the house. I looked through one of her file boxes — almost every coupon in it had expired, but Mrs. Gizzale never seemed to slow down, and after dinner she would sit down at the table, scissors in hand, and begin shearing paper.

Raintree introduced me and handed Mr. Gizzale some papers to sign. Mr. Gizzale looked as if he were used to the process and walked the papers over to the dining room table. Mrs. Gizzale had been doing her evening clipping, and he had to push some pages around to make a space. "We have just finished our evening meal," Mr. Gizzale said. "Has she eaten her dinner?"

Raintree looked embarrassed, because he knew that I hadn't, but I said, "I'm not very hungry."

Mr. Gizzale looked up at me. "Yes, I should think not." He finished signing the papers and asked Raintree, point-blank, "Is she to leave the house at all?"

Raintree frowned. "Well, there are no charges pending against Patty, but we would rather she not go back to school right now — there might be problems."

Mr. Gizzale nodded that final-looking nod of his. "I understand."

"What about my stuff?" I asked.

Raintree squinted at me. "What?"

"My clothes and stuff. They even took my purse. I don't have anything to wear."

Raintree looked annoyed. "I'll try to get in touch with the FBI people to see if it's possible to get a bag for you."

"Why wouldn't it be? It's my stuff."

Raintree squirmed a bit. "I'm sure we can fix you up, Patty."

"I'm going to need some things."

"I'll take care of it in the morning."

"Whatever."

On his way to the door Raintree handed me his

card with the telephone number where I could reach him. "If you have any difficulties, Patty, be sure to call."

I nodded. Whatever else might happen, I was not going to be calling Raintree. I needed to get in touch with Kimmers.

Mr. Gizzale let Raintree out of the house, then turned to me. "That was incredibly rude," he said.

"What?" I didn't understand.

"You will be taken care of here."

"I just wanted my clothes."

"And you thought that we would not take care of you?"

I didn't know what to say, but Mr. Gizzale didn't give me the chance, anyway. He told me to sit down and listen. I looked around the living room, which was done over in modern plastic, and hesitated. All of the furniture, including the two standing lamps, was wrapped in clear plastic covers. To keep the dirt off, I suppose, but it looked as if the furniture hadn't been cleaned since long before they thought to wrap it up in plastic. Actually, the furniture looked as if it hadn't been cleaned since long before plastic was *invented*.

I sat down in a plastic-wrapped chair and looked up.

"We have certain rules for the children of our house," said Mr. Gizzale. "We have three grown children of our own, but we are old now and do not like noise. You must try to be quiet."

I nodded; that was reasonable.

"Also," he said, "the telephone. You may not use the telephone at any time, except with one of us here to tell you that you may. I am sorry, but we have had some bad experiences with the long-distance bill, and social services does not pay for phone calls."

I shrugged. I would be out searching for a phone booth real soon.

"Bedtime is nine o'clock. We do not watch television here."

Ouch!

I wondered if the real reason they would not let me use the telephone was germs. A spray can of disinfectant was posted near the receiver. I once read about this millionaire who became a germ freak but still wouldn't allow anyone to change his bedsheets for months at a time. That was what the Gizzales reminded me of.

"I will show you where you sleep."

Mr. Gizzale led me down the musky hall, past the bathroom, and right into a cheap cartoonist's nightmare. At fifteen years old, I was about to be locked in a room covered with bunnies and bluebirds. The bedspread featured a huge cartoon rabbit wearing coveralls and holding a sunflower.

I suspected that the Gizzales had not been expecting a dangerous teenage thug like myself.

I must be dangerous. It had taken four agents of the Federal Bureau of Investigation to drag me from the J. T. Kreuger Senior High School parking lot to

South Bend and this travesty of justice. The Sandman's daughter. How could I explain to these creeps that I never even knew the Sandman?

All I knew was my dad.

And as far as I was concerned, it could still have been just a complicated set-up, like something on television. Somebody somewhere really hated and despised my dad and was doing all of this. Who could we turn to for help?

"Hey," I said to Mr. Gizzale. "I really am a little hungry now."

"We have finished our evening meal."

"Yeah, but —"

"You will enjoy breakfast," he said in that final tone of his.

Okay, I thought. "I have to find a phone booth," I said. "I've got some calls to make."

"It is nearly eight-thirty in the evening," he said. "It is best that you should stay inside. You may read for a while if you like."

I frowned. "What?"

"There are books and magazines in the house."

"No, I mean why do I have to stay in? It's early. I really do have to make some calls."

"Not this evening."

"Can I use your phone?"

"Not this evening."

At this point I did not feel like a rude guest. I felt like a prisoner. "Look, do you know what happened to me today?"

"It is not my business."

"I'm Patty Meely, and I —"

"I know who you are."

"Yeah, well, the FBI grabbed my dad for some reason, and I don't understand what is going on. I don't have any clothes, I don't have anything of mine, I'm just here. I'm here, and I need to call some people and talk about this."

"Not this evening." He started to leave.

"You can't just lock me up," I said. He seemed shocked. "I'm not in jail."

"Not yet." He nodded.

I didn't like the way he said that, or the smirk on his face, either. "What do you mean by that?"

"We will discuss all of this in the morning, perhaps," he said. "This is quiet time."

"I don't feel like being quiet."

"The authorities will decide tomorrow whom you may call," he said. "I will speak no further on this." He started to back out into the hallway again. "You may cross the hall to use the bathroom if you need to. Otherwise it is best that you stay in your room for the rest of the evening. My wife will talk to you in the morning about your other needs."

"The only thing I need is to call some people."

"Good night." He pulled the door shut behind him as he backed out. I turned away in disgust and slugged that stupid rabbit on the bed.

It had been only a few hours since the guys in the gray cars and suits had snatched Dad, but it seemed

I had always been alone. I was almost getting used to the coldness of it. First the FBI agents, then Raintree, and now the Gizzales. I didn't mean anything to them. I was just a case.

It occurred to me that I had almost never been alone. There was always Dad or Kimmers or Larry or Mark or some party or school function or somewhere to hang out.

If this was the real world, I wanted no part of it.

I was sitting on the edge of that ridiculous rabbit bed when I heard an odd noise. A sort of clump, clickity-clickity, and a scratching sound. *Terrific*, I thought as I looked around. To top it all off, rats. No doubt big and fiendishly hairy rats. So I was looking around the room for the source of the scratching when something furry brushed up against my ankle, and I yelped. The noise I made was probably more of a shriek or a scream, but most of the sound was snarled halfway up and lodged in my throat, producing the classic Patty Meely Yelp.

I shivered and jumped and fell backward. That was when I first saw the cat. He crawled out from beneath the bed, sat down, and turned to face me. He licked some dust from his fur and then looked up, as if to ask, "So how long are you in for, kid?"

I tried to relax. "I just aged two years because of you, cat."

He continued to groom himself.

"Do you mind if I pet you?"

He didn't answer, so I took it as an okay. I leaned

forward and stroked his head. He clicked on the purr box. Into medium, I guess. That cat had the loudest purr I have ever heard. I started scratching behind his ears, and he sounded like a broken outboard motor. I was sure Mr. Gizzale was going to come charging in to remind me that evening was "quiet time."

"I need to get out of here to make a call, cat," I said as I stroked him. "Any suggestions?"

He did not leap up to reveal any secret panels or passages in the walls, so I was forced to wait until the Gizzales went to sleep. Then I would slip out of the window for a while.

They locked up the house precisely at nine, and Mr. Gizzale knocked on my door as his wife was turning off the lights. "I see you have found the cat," he noted.

I nodded. "What's his name?"

"He is called Mr. Wise and he is an old cat. Ancient He should not be excited, so do not play too roughly with him."

"How old is he?"

"Old."

I shrugged, and Mr. Gizzale informed me it was lights out on C Block. He paused in the doorway, as if waiting for me to slip immediately into unconsciousness. "Just a minute," I said.

"Nine o'clock is bedtime."

"Well, I'm not getting undressed with you standing there watching."

He frowned and told me that was not his intention. "You can undress in the dark," he said as he clicked off the light and pulled the door shut. I heard more doors shutting and some muttering. After about fifteen minutes the house grew quiet. I did not undress but sat in the dark, petting the cat. I waited another fifteen minutes and then put Mr. Wise down on the edge of the bed, where he curled up into a ball and promptly dozed off. I walked to the window and examined it.

It was a typical old-fashioned sash window, so I slid open the lock at the top and tugged it up gently. At first it stuck, since it had been partially painted shut, but finally it gave and slid open stiffly with a few squeaks. I held my breath and listened for any sudden noises in the house, such as Mr. Gizzale rising from bed to investigate.

Nothing.

"Keep watch," I whispered to Mr. Wise, but he was sound asleep at his post.

I managed to crawl out the window and leap into the hedge without totally destroying myself. I was jabbed and stuck by the hedge needles, but I pulled away. The night was cool and I slunk out of the yard, trying to avoid making any noises that would cause Mr. Gizzale to think there was a prowler. I walked quickly to the corner, then turned down the street.

I was not exactly in the best of neighborhoods, but my biggest problem was finding a telephone booth. I figured that almost every neighborhood in the world had a twenty-four-hour deli or grocery or gas station, so it was probably only a question of walking far enough to find it. That was what I was doing when I came across the old man and the dog.

The dog was a mixed-breed shepherd with gray and black fur and a bad temper. He came out from behind the tree he was examining and blocked my path. He was not on a leash. The dog growled from low in his throat and took one, two, three steps, and stopped. I froze.

The old man walking the dog was bent and had a patchy gray beard and a mane of shaggy white hair. He was wrapped in a slightly tattered green army field jacket and wore jeans and sneakers. "Nice night," he remarked.

"Definitely." It was a stupid remark, but it was all I could say. The animal kept up his growl. I could picture it now: dragged to South Bend by agents of the FBI just so I could be mauled by some crazed animal. "I don't think he likes me," I said.

"Eh, what?"

"Your dog."

"Eh?" He shrugged. "Not my dog, no sir. Wouldn't have a terrible dog like that."

"Oh." I nodded.

"Shut up!" He balled a fist and banged the dog harshly atop the snout. The dog nipped at his hand but stopped growling and returned to the tree.

"Eh, bad animal, I think," said the old man.

"Is there a phone booth around here?" I asked.

41

"Why?"

"What?" I was confused.

He shook his head. "Phone at the service station. Clean Mike's. None at the bar. Not that works, anyway."

"A service station?"

"That's what I said, eh?"

"Where is it?"

"I know you don't know where it is. The dog is stupid, but he knows where it is. Down the street some blocks. I ain't counting how many. You go figure if you need to. Stay clear of that bar, you hear me?"

I nodded.

"Stay clear of that bar, you hear?" He demanded this a bit louder now.

"I hear you, yes."

"Don't worry about the dog. He's old. Some sick, I guess. Don't know what to do with sick dogs."

"I'm sorry."

"Don't be sorry until you have to. There's always more reason to be sorry." He kept walking up the street with his dog.

I hurried along until I came to a well-lit tavern on the corner of a sad-looking street. I could see a gas station about a block and a half farther down, so I took the old man's advice and crossed the street to avoid the bar. Loud country and western music was seeping out of the place, the kind my dad liked to listen to. I walked on to the station, and there was a battered telephone booth out front. I dialed the operator to make a collect call to Kimmers' house.

The phone rang twice, and Mom answered and accepted the charges. I say "Mom" answered, because I have been calling Kimmers' mother "Mom" for as long as I can remember. I have spent so much time at Kimmers' house, sleeping over and cooking and goofing off, that it's almost like her mother really is my mom. She sure yells at me like she thinks she is.

"Patty?" she asked. "Is that you?"

"Yeah, Mom. I think I'm in trouble."

"We saw. It was all over the television tonight."

"It can't be true," I said. "There's something wrong. Somebody is wrong."

"I don't know. Did you see the news story?"

"No," I admitted. "Can I come over and stay with you?" Actually, I don't even know why I bothered to ask. I should have just said that I was on my way over, or asked for a ride.

I felt a chill and a coldness growing in my stomach when I heard Mom say, "Well, I don't know about that."

"Why don't you know?"

"Those people who took your daddy away today were FBI men and United States marshals."

"I know who they were."

"Well, maybe we should wait and see what is happening here."

"Mom, they took me to a foster home. I'm in South Bend, with strangers. I haven't got any clothes. I

43

haven't got anything. I want to be somewhere."

"I know you do, baby, but this is pretty big stuff. Maybe it would be best if you stayed where they put you until we find out what's going on."

"How am I supposed to know what's going on? They haven't told me anything — all they want to do is ask questions."

"Maybe you should answer their questions, Patty."

"What?"

"They mentioned that money on television, Patty. Maybe it would be best if you told them about it."

"What? I don't know anything about any money, Mom. I just want to leave here."

"You can maybe call back in a few days and we'll see about getting you out of there."

I was nervesick now: My stomach was a ball of worms and I was shaking and my arms and legs felt numb. "Can I talk to Kimmers?"

"Yes, she's here." I heard Mom tell Kimmers: "Don't be long, it's collect."

I felt even sicker about that.

"Hello?"

"Kimmers, I think it's bad."

"Where are you?"

"I'm in South Bend in a foster home. Can you believe that? Me in a foster home?"

"Wow."

"I think these people are all crazy."

"It's in the news, Patty."

"What are they saying?"

44

"That your dad was a spy and he broke out of prison twenty years ago and there was a lot of money and you and your mom knew about it."

"I didn't know anything!" I said. "It can't be true if I was supposed to know it." I was adding up that last thought in my head. It made sense: If the whole thing could not have happened without my knowing it, then it must not have really happened. I told this to Kimmers. "Maybe it's all a bad mistake."

"They had old movies of your dad, Patty."

"How can that be?"

"It's him," she said. "And they're all over your house, too."

"What?"

"We drove by. It looks like they're taking it apart. They're tearing the walls out, the floors, everything. They have a rope around the front and they're digging up your yard. They're looking for stuff."

"What stuff?"

"The money and other stuff, I guess."

I shook my head and said, "They're not going to find anything."

"You never know, Patty."

I guess I let myself sound a little angry then. "Kimmers, this is my dad we're talking about. Not some television story. You've known my dad almost your whole life."

"You never really know anyone, Patty. We're all strangers. Some of us just keep more secrets."

I didn't say anything.

45

Kimmers finally asked, "So what are you going to do?"

"What can I do?"

She had no immediate suggestions.

I was thinking about Rye Springs.

Rye Springs is a rock-filled cove near the Indiana Dunes on the lakefront. It is sheltered from the worst of the winds and concealed from all avenues of approach, which means simply that nobody can see into Rye Springs. The cove was on my mind because of the time I ran away from home when I was twelve. I ran away for a lot of reasons which seemed important then, but mostly I left because I was having problems with guys and such and was missing having a mother, a real mother to talk to. Kimmers' mom was trying to help, but I was feeling the gaps in my life, and one afternoon after school Dad and I got into a stupid argument, so I took off. At nine that night he finally found me at the Marquette Mall, walking the aisles in Sears. I was scared he would be crazy, but he wasn't. The next day was Saturday, and he took me to Rye Springs, where we flipped pebbles into the pond. We talked a lot about everything, but he finished by saying, "Sometimes you have to run away. I know that. But when you really feel like you have to hide yourself from the world, come here. That way I'll know where to find you."

This time, though, he wouldn't be able to take me home.

Kimmers was still on the line, and I guess Mom

was reminding her that it was a long distance collect call. Kimmers stayed on for just a while longer, though. She asked, "Where are you going to go?"

"Go?" I thought about it. "Where can anyone really go these days?"

This time Kimmers said nothing. I knew she was embarrassed, so I said goodbye and hung up. I thought again about Rye Springs, but I was not prepared for everything that hiding out in a rock cove entails. Besides, there was really only one way to find out the truth about what was happening.

I had to go back to the Gizzales'.

FOUR

Mr. Gizzale came in early to get me out of bed. He seemed annoyed and told me some FBI men were waiting for me in the living room. I hadn't bothered to get undressed before going to sleep, and when I sat up, dropping the covers in front of me, Mr. Gizzale looked almost disappointed. He turned and shuffled out of the room. I stood up, slipped my shoes back on, and dragged myself across the hall to the bathroom. I felt filthy, but I didn't even have a change of clothes.

I closed the bathroom door and started to wash as best I could, but the face in the bathroom mirror was horrible to look at. My eyes were hollow and bloodshot, I was pale, and my hair was totally trashed. I washed my face and stuck out my tongue at the image looking back at me. My teeth were wearing little wool sweaters, but I had no toothbrush, so I just rinsed my mouth with some cold water and went out to the living room.

Walkins and Munroe, the thugs who had grabbed me in front of the school, were standing there waiting. They were still wearing their conservative gray suits, so I took the opportunity to be a wise guy. "I see they didn't let you guys change clothes, either."

Walkins and Munroe just frowned, the remark obviously sailing right over their heads. Walkins stepped forward and told me I was scheduled for another interview with Special Agent Helker. My stomach was groaning: I had not eaten anything since lunch the day before. I mentioned this to Walkins. "Could I get some breakfast first?"

Walkins looked uncomfortable. Then he pulled his face tough. "I'm sorry. We have to get you to the Federal Building before seven-thirty."

I nodded. "Could you at least describe what you guys ate this morning? I've forgotten exactly what food looks like."

Walkins turned to Mr. Gizzale. "Do you think you could make her some toast? She can eat it on the ride over."

Mr. Gizzale nodded and disappeared into the kitchen. I shook my head, apologizing. "I hope I don't throw today's schedule too far off."

Mr. Gizzale quickly reappeared with two slices of dry white toast, and we left the house.

I ate that toast on the ride downtown, doing my best to inflict some guilt on Walkins and his silent sidekick. I doubt the guilt attack worked. Walkins looked like the type of guy who has his conscience

49

surgically removed at a very young age. They drove into the parking garage of the Federal Building again and escorted me back up to the fourth floor.

INTERROGATION TWO had changed some since the evening before. Another table had been brought in and a reel-to-reel tape recorder set up on it. I assumed this was meant to replace Marshal Rogers' small cassette player. An electric coffee pot filled the room with a warm morning smell, and a box of doughnuts had been torn into. The dictionary had been removed.

Marshal Rogers was sitting at the desk with a copy of the Chicago *Tribune*. At first I figured what he was reading had to do with Dad, but he muttered something about the Bears, and I realized he was scanning the sports page. I closed the door behind me and he looked up, almost smiling. "Good morning," he said.

I frowned. "You have got to be kidding."

He shrugged. "Sorry." He gestured over to the doughnuts and told me to help myself, which I did. I was midway through the second one when Rogers told me to sit down. "Would you like to look at the paper?"

"Is there anything about my dad in it?"

"Ah — I can't let you look at that section," he said awkwardly. "I thought you might like to read the comics, though."

I shook my head. "I've lost my sense of humor."

"You'll get it back."

I shook my head again.

"Ah, you would be surprised." Rogers poured himself a cup of coffee. "You know, I have a daughter about your age. Her name is Katie. She's sixteen."

I opened my eyes wide.

Rogers laughed. "I only look as if I'm as old as the hills. Really I'm not. Can you guess how old I am?"

I didn't want to, but he stayed silent, waiting. Finally I said, "Forty-one."

Rogers laughed harder. "You meant to say fifty."

I blushed. I meant to say fifty-five.

"You're wrong," he said. "Thirty-six."

"Really?" I couldn't help being surprised. "Wow."

He nodded. "It's this job that takes it out of you. Lousy hours, fast food all the time—I must drink sixty cups of coffee a day."

"Why don't you quit?"

"Because I'm doing something meaningful."

I nodded. "Is having me here meaningful?"

He sighed and took another sip of his coffee. "That's not for me to say."

The door popped open then, and Helker walked in. He was carrying a small box, the kind you might find out behind a busy supermarket. He set it down by his chair, pulled open the top, reached in, and came out with my purse. "I thought you might like this back," he said as he handed it to me.

I accepted it and looked inside.

Helker smiled. "Everything's there. I won't insult your intelligence by telling you we didn't look, but I will promise that we didn't take anything."

51

I zipped the purse back up and looked at him.

"Inventory complete?" he asked. "Or have we reached a certain level of trust?"

"My stuff is still there," I said.

Helker nodded. "I've got a few more things here for you. Stuff we found at your house: a couple of changes of clothing, some toilet articles, your diary —"

I jerked forward, not even thinking. "Give me that, you creep!"

Helker didn't try to keep me from the box; he just stepped out of my path. "A bit embarrassed, are we not?"

I sorted through the contents of the box. The clothes and other things were there, but not the diary. I looked up at Helker. "Where is it?"

He shrugged. "I'll have it for you in a few minutes. It's being photocopied."

"You can't do that."

"At this stage, Patty, I can do almost anything I want."

I sank back in my seat, across the table from Rogers. He would not meet my eyes. Helker took his seat now, between me and Rogers. He started the tape recorder and pulled the microphone to the center of the table. "I don't know why you're so upset," he said. "As far as diaries go it was pretty dull stuff. I almost dozed off, except for the part about that boy last summer —"

"That was private." I tried to make my voice sound very, very cold.

Helker smiled. "Let's talk about some private things, shall we?"

I shook my head. "I want a lawyer."

"Perhaps later."

"What?"

"You don't understand, Patty. You are not yet charged with any crime, so you are not entitled to have a lawyer present."

"That's not what Agent Walkins said."

"That's what *Special Agent* Helker says, so believe it."

"What if I just refuse to say anything?"

"Then I suspect we'll be here quite a long time."

I frowned. "What about my rights?"

"When you turn eighteen maybe you'll decide to sue me. Until then I'm not too worried."

I sat back in my chair, dumbfounded.

Helker consulted a handwritten list he produced from his pocket. "First of all, let us talk about the money."

"What money?"

Helker smiled again, twitching as he had the day before. "Did you read the clippings I left with you yesterday?"

"Yeah — a bunch of garbage."

Helker dropped the smile. He made the next sound like an aside. "The sad thing is, of course, that you no longer believe that, do you, Patty?"

I said nothing.

Helker nodded. "Tell me about the money."

"I don't know anything about any money."

"Okay. Are you familiar with the term 'obstruction of justice'?"

I shook my head.

"It means withholding evidence, or by any other means of commission or omission attempting to interfere with the investigation of a crime. Obstruction of justice is a felony."

"I really don't know anything."

"Okay." He stood up and began to pace the room. "Let me tell you what the situation is. As we speak, your father, Mr. Casper Pelling, is being transported to Leavenworth Federal Penitentiary in Kansas."

"What about his trial?"

"Trial? What trial? Your father got his trial twenty years ago. He's just another escaped con going back to the joint."

The image of my dad in prison chilled me.

"As for you, Patricia Pelling, you are proving more difficult. We're still trying to unravel all of the running that your father did. It's hard to figure out just who your relatives really are. A lot of cranks are coming out of the woodwork, claiming to be long-lost aunts and uncles. They're all looking for publicity. We even have three ladies who say they're your mother."

I looked away.

Helker's voice suddenly came across very cold, very hard. "If it were up to me, Patricia Pelling, you would get your lawyer. I would love to prosecute you on this."

"On what?"

"Don't act so innocent. I'm fairly sure we could nail you on one or two interesting little felonies."

"If you feel froggy, jump."

Helker smirked and then slowly shook his head. "The district attorney feels that any prosecution against you right now would prove very unpopular. He is willing to back off. Provided, of course, that you find it within yourself to help us out."

"Even if I did know anything, I wouldn't tell you," I said. "Why should I? I'm not as scared as I was yesterday, Helker, and your threats are starting to get dull. Either throw me in jail or ask me something else."

"What should I ask you?"

"I get straight A's in history. Ask me something about the American Revolution."

"How about Benedict Arnold?"

I looked across to Rogers. "You guys took my father away and dragged me to a foster home. My life is ruined. What else do you want from me?"

Rogers finally spoke. "As far as the United States Marshals Service is concerned, Patty, we don't want anything more from you. We just want to help you find your proper family." Rogers stood up. "If the FBI has other concerns, I'm sure Agent Helker will make these very clear now."

Rogers was staring directly at Helker. There seemed to be a challenge of some sort. Helker looked rattled. "The capture of escaped fugitives is the responsibility of the Marshals Service," he said. "The FBI investigates federal crimes."

"Do you have any evidence that a federal crime has been committed?" Rogers asked.

Helker didn't move for a moment; then he shook his head. "No. Not yet. But the investigation isn't over."

"A formality. What do you plan to do with Patty?"

"There is nothing to do with her," Helker said. "We're just taking the opportunity to question her while we wait for her next of kin to be located."

Rogers switched off the tape recorder. "Patty, this interview is over. If you don't mind, I'd like you to wait here while I have a word with Agent Helker outside. Bob? Could I talk to you a minute?"

Helker bit his lip and nodded.

They went out into the hall and pulled the door closed behind them. I went over to the tape recorder and switched it to REWIND. The counter numbers spun backward until I stopped it again. Then I put the lever on PLAY, and my voice came out of the speaker: "*not as scared as I was yesterday, Helker, and your threats are starting to get dull. Either throw me in jail —*"

The door snapped open again and I turned the recorder off. Marshal Rogers eased back in. He pushed the door shut behind him and sighed. "I'm sorry about all of that, Patty. Like I said, I have a daughter of my own."

I didn't say anything.

He shrugged. "Bob is a little insensitive sometimes."

"Sometimes?"

"He's one of the best investigators I ever met. He pulled the Pelling file two years ago just for something to do on a slow night. Right now he's sort of caught up in his own success. He has a bit of a big head over the whole thing, but I think he'll be all right."

"He's a creep."

Rogers chuckled. "Yeah, maybe he is."

"A genuine nasty."

Rogers shrugged. "He found a way to do his job right, and I guess that requires you to be a genuine nasty. Myself, I never get over the guilt."

"So you're not a good U.S. marshal?"

"I'm not a good detective. There are other things I'm good at."

"So do I get to leave now?"

"You're going back to the foster home until we can locate your family for you."

I grimaced. "Isn't there anything you can do to get me out of there?"

Rogers looked puzzled. "What do you mean?"

"That guy Gizzale is another genuine nasty. Besides, I have friends I would rather stay with."

"That's a little out of my hands."

"Could you try?"

He hesitated, then nodded. "Yeah. I'll try."

"Thank you for helping me."

He nodded again, then frowned. "I'm sorry about everything that's happened to you, Patty. I really am. But I hope you understand most of it is really your father's doing, not ours. I know that's kind of hard to figure right now, but someday you'll realize that and not hold everything against us."

I shook my head. "Can I go now?"

"Yeah. I'll get a deputy marshal to drive you over. I want to get you away from the FBI."

"Thank you."

Marshal Rogers started to say something else but the door opened again. Helker rushed back in, looking somehow pleased with himself. I could tell he'd found some reason not to let me leave — and I was right. He said, "I think we need Patty to wait around a while."

"What?" Rogers went tense. "Why?"

"Let's talk in the hall."

"I'm just about through talking to you in hallways, Bob."

"Okay, fine. Casper Pelling seems to have a talent. Somehow he managed to get away from the U.S. marshals who were escorting him to the airport." Helker seemed to emphasize the words *U.S. marshals*.

Rogers asked immediately, "Was anyone hurt?"

"No. He just walked away."

"What do you mean, 'walked away'? Wasn't he in handcuffs?"

"Apparently not."

"How long ago did this happen?"

"Less than fifteen minutes. Looks like I'm back on the case again."

"Negative. This is no dead file, Bob. I trust you to stand back. Where did it happen?"

"The escort pulled over at a truck stop on the Interstate. I don't have all the details, but I guess somebody wasn't watching where they were supposed to be."

"Save the judgments — just tell me what you know."

"We know what he was wearing, and I've already checked to make sure the right notifications were made. The highway patrol, sheriffs' departments, my people. . . ." Helker smiled. "Oh, and I did notify you."

Rogers ignored that. "What about the press?"

Helker shook his head.

"Do it now."

Helker snarled. "Speaking of 'just abouts,' I think I've just about had enough of taking orders from you, Walter."

"I think you're just about to lose this assignment, Helker."

"I think somebody is. I don't know if it will be me or not. But, hey, I'll call the newspapers. I might enjoy explaining how the marshals lost him again." Helker paused in the doorway and gestured at me. "Don't get too excited, Patricia Pelling. We'll have him back in custody within the hour."

"Don't be so confident," said Rogers.

"Why not?"

"You seem to forget. He's good at this."

Helker frowned. "Just try to make sure that she doesn't disappear on you, too."

The door closed behind him.

Rogers sighed and looked over at me.

My mind was going absolutely crazy. First my dad was arrested in front of the high school and now he had escaped somewhere along the Interstate? My dad, an escaped-convict spy? What was the truth now, anyway?

I supposed there was really only one truth anymore, and I said it to Rogers: "I really am alone now."

He nodded absently. "I'll have somebody bring you something to eat. Something to read."

"I don't get to leave?"

"Not right now."

"I have a question."

Rogers said, "I have to go accomplish some things."

"You have to go catch my dad?"

Rogers didn't answer. He just looked at me.

I thought a minute. "If you had to kill my father

to keep him from getting away again, would you do it?"

For a second Rogers looked as if he were going to answer the question, but finally he didn't. He turned away and left the room, closing the door firmly behind him.

FIVE

Shortly after a graysuit brought me a plate of terrible food for lunch, Helker returned. He asked me once again if I had any ideas as to where Dad might be going. It was a question he had been asking all morning. After almost six hours of searching they were apparently no closer to finding Dad then they had been in the minutes following his escape.

I told him no. My answer was not exactly the truth. I had some very definite thoughts as to where Dad might go to hide out in the daylight, but Helker was a creep. Besides, it is impossible not to root for your own father, no matter what terrible things have been said about him.

So Helker asked me again and I said no again. I was beginning to grow comfortable with the lie.

Scraping my fork across the plate, I managed to mush up the food without actually eating any. "What exactly is this?" I asked. "FBI Surprise?"

Helker ignored my crack. "You don't have any thoughts as to where he might hide?"

"Can I get a soda?" I said, deadpan. "Or some milk? I need something to wash this horrible stuff down."

Helker said nothing else and left in a huff.

Shortly after that, they decided to allow me to go back to the Gizzales'. A United States marshal was assigned to drive me, and he escorted me from INTERROGATION TWO down to the parking garage. The door of his blue car said U.S. GOVERNMENT — FOR OFFICIAL USE ONLY.

"Am I an official use?"

"Must be. Government regulations." He unlocked the car.

"Can I ride up front with you?"

"Absolutely. But you have to fasten your seat belt. Government regulations."

I nodded and climbed in beside him. "Are you my guard?"

"I'm your driver. Do you need a guard?"

"What's your name?"

"Mitch."

"Mitch?"

"Mitch Doonegan."

"You mean it's not *Agent* Doonegan?"

"What do you mean *Agent*? You mean like CIA agent?"

"FBI."

"Losers. I'm a United States marshal. And my name is Mitch."

"Glad to meet you, Marshal Mitch."

"Likewise."

"I'm Patty. It's just Patty for now, as my last name is currently in dispute."

"I know."

"You do?"

"Yeah. They have to tell me who I'm driving. It's a —"

"Let me guess. A government regulation."

"Exactly." He looked over at me. "Where do you stand on cheeseburgers?"

"Depends. Where do you stand on onions?"

"Fine, just as long as you stay on your own side of the car."

"I promise. I'm starving."

"I thought you might be. I saw what they brought you for lunch."

Marshal Mitch started the car. He drove us across town to a Big Jay Burgers drive-through. I ordered a Super Jay with cheese, lots of onions, and some french fries. Marshal Mitch made a few bad-breath jokes and then ordered some onion rings to go with his burger. "Self-defense," he explained. We got our food and he pulled the car off to the side of the parking lot.

After a few mouthfuls of burger he looked over at me. "I guess this has been really rough on you."

"Is that a question?"

"No. Just an awkward remark."

I continued eating. After a moment I asked, "So how long have you been a marshal?"

"About two and a half years. Why?"

"You look young."

"Yeah. I'm new around here."

I nodded. "So what about Rogers?"

"Are you kidding? He's been around since about six months before they installed the dirt."

"So why are you being so nice to me?"

"Why shouldn't I be nice? You didn't do anything wrong."

"I'm glad somebody thinks so."

He finished his burger and wiped his mouth with a paper napkin. "Now your father, on the other hand, he is a rough character. A real genuine nasty."

My ears perked at that. "A what?"

"A real rough character."

I took another small bite. "What do you mean 'rough'?"

"Violent."

I chilled. "Violent?"

He paused. "Well, I probably shouldn't be talking about this with you. I meant the first jailbreak."

"So what about the first jailbreak?"

"People were hurt."

"What?"

"The 1966 breakout. I figured they would have rammed that one into your head by now. Casper Pelling hurt some people."

The question at first choked in my throat, but I finally managed to whisper it. "How . . . how badly were they hurt?"

"Well, they weren't dead, but one of them was close. Your dad hit him square in the back with a lead pipe."

I stopped eating.

"Hey, I'm sorry. . . ."

I bit into my lower lip. "Can we go now?"

"Sure. I'm sorry. I thought you knew about that."

"No."

He nodded and started the car. After a while he switched on the radio, and finally he spoke. "Hey, if you want somebody to talk to besides those losers downtown . . . well, you can talk to me."

I was lost again. "What?"

"I know it must hurt a lot."

"How do you know anything?"

"I think about it. You think you know somebody for years and suddenly it all changes. It turns out it was all just a lie."

"How do I know it was all just a lie?"

He looked at me.

"How? How do I know it was just a lie?" I repeated. "He said he loved me. Am I supposed to believe that was a lie just because you guys tell me it was? Were all those feelings false just because you guys say his name was?"

Marshal Mitch frowned. "You said yourself he always seemed to hide things from you."

"So what if he did — What?"

"You said —"

Now I definitely felt very strange. "When did I say any of that?"

"Well . . . you didn't exactly say . . ."

Something else dawned on me. "When did I ever call anyone a genuine nasty around you?"

"I don't —"

"What did you do to me?"

He blushed then, turned away, and kept his eyes squarely fixed on the road. "It was your diary. I read those things in your diary."

"Oh, my God."

"I had to, Patty. It wasn't like I was invading your privacy —"

"Oh, my God."

"— It was just my job, Patty."

"All of it? You guys read all of it?"

"I —"

"How many copies did you make?"

"Just two. For the files. We —"

"Did you like it? Did it entertain you? Cheap thrills?"

"I'm sorry, Patty. We had to read it."

"Why? You said yourself I didn't do anything wrong."

Marshal Mitch didn't speak for a minute. Then he asked, "Do you know where he is, Patty?"

I shivered, this time all the way from my toes to the top of my rattled head. Among other things, I was thinking about what I had written about Mark in my diary. About a dream I had about him. "Is that why they told you to take me for burgers? To see if I would slip up and answer your questions?"

"We need to know, Patty."

"Forget you!"

He seemed offended and drove to the Gizzales' in silence. Mr. Gizzale greeted us at the door, seeming none too pleased at my return. I guess he was surprised to see that I wasn't rotting away in a dark dungeon somewhere. No doubt he had assumed me gone for good. He probably even burned the sheets off the rabbit bed. He turned to Marshal Mitch after closing the front door and said, "I thought perhaps other arrangements were being made for her."

Marshal Mitch shrugged. "I'm just the driver, sir. You can call social services if you want."

"I will."

Mr. Gizzale moved off, and Marshal Mitch stood beside me, waiting. "Anything else you want to say to me?"

"Lots. But it's all in bad taste."

He nodded absently and Mr. Gizzale returned, looking, if possible, even more unhappy. It had been confirmed: I would be residing at the Gizzale house for at least another night. Marshal Mitch said his goodbyes. I dragged my box of supplies back to the cartoon room and unpacked it.

Finally I had a chance to take a bath and get cleaned up. Once I got into the tub, I scrubbed myself nearly raw. I was just drying off when I heard voices arguing in the living room. Mr. Gizzale and a woman. Not his wife. A reporter.

The news had found me.

"Please, sir, just a few questions —"

"Please, no, get out of this house —"

"Where is she?"

"No reporters! Please!"

"Patty! Patty Pelling!"

They were arguing in the living room and I shrunk back against the bathroom door. My hair was wet, an uncombed, tangled mess, and I suddenly felt very frightened. Patty Meely did not exist anymore, and Patty Pelling had a lot to answer for.

The reporter was asking, "How do you feel having the daughter of a convicted Soviet spy in your house?"

"I do not feel. I do what I have to do."

"Do you believe the reports that she had no idea who her father really was?"

"I can't answer that."

I pulled open the bathroom door and shouted down the hall. It was more for Mr. Gizzale than for the reporter. "I'll answer that!"

The reporter — a red-haired woman in a tan suit — raced down the hall toward me. "Patricia Pelling?"

"Meely. Patricia Meely."

"Your father is Casper Pelling?"

"My dad is Doug Meely."

"Who was arrested yesterday on the steps of Kreuger High School in Michigan City?"

Reluctantly I nodded.

"And you are saying that you had no idea that your father was a previously convicted Soviet spy?"

"I haven't said anything yet."

"So you did know?"

"I don't understand any of it."

"What about the money?"

"Can I just ask you a question first?"

This startled her. She stood up a little straighter. "What's the question?"

"Who are you?"

"My name is Alice Wyatt. I'm a reporter for the Associated Press."

"What is that?"

"A wire service."

"A what?"

"Uh . . . we provide news for newspapers and radio stations across the country."

I nodded.

"So what about the money?" she asked.

"Did you know that they read my diary?" I countered.

"What?"

"The FBI photocopied and read my diary this morning."

Alice Wyatt seemed to be hanging on my every word. "And?"

"What do you mean 'And'?"

"What did they find?"

I frowned. "You people are all crazy."

70

"Patty, are you saying that you know nothing about the money?"

"What money?"

"The hundred thousand dollars."

"I wish I had it so I could hire a good lawyer."

Alice Wyatt smiled. "You know you're not exactly how your friends described you."

"What? What do you mean?"

"We talked to some of your friends from school this morning. . . ."

"Kimmers? Did you talk to Kimmers?"

Now Alice Wyatt looked *really* interested. "Who?"

"Never mind." I was starting to learn when to close my mouth.

"Your friends described you as quiet, sensitive."

"Who?"

"I don't remember names, exactly."

"They probably weren't really my friends."

"Who really were your friends?"

"I thought you already knew that."

Alice Wyatt smiled again; this time it was as if she were clenching her teeth.

"I'm sorry if I don't meet your profile."

She scribbled in her notebook.

"What are you writing?"

"Just some notes."

"Notes about me?"

"That's right."

"Why?"

"People are interested."

"Is it any of their business?"

"It's news."

"If they kill my father today will you be back tonight to ask me how I feel about it?"

"How *would* you feel about it?"

"That's sick."

"Maybe it is. Look around you, Patty. It's a sick world."

I took a breath. "Maybe it is. But until yesterday afternoon I never had to know about it."

"Would you consider yourself sheltered?"

"I'm lonely. I would consider myself alone."

Alice Wyatt asked one final question. "Do you have any place to go? Anybody to go to?"

I thought about that. I was still thinking when Mr. Gizzale came down the hall with a policeman who calmly escorted Alice Wyatt out of the house. I thought about it long after the sun had gone down and I was hiding beneath the covers in the cartoon room. Mr. Wise the cat was asleep on the floor beside me, and I sat up in bed, looking out the window again. The streetlamp on the corner cast everything into dark shadow. It was after eleven o'clock, and I was thinking about Rye Springs again. Not realistically, but more out of worried curiosity.

In spite of everything, I was still thinking of my father as Dad and not as some creature they called Casper Pelling. He was still Doug Meely, the guy who worked at the steel mill. He was still the man who walked around shopping malls with me so I could pick out my own birthday present. I suppose part of my reasoning for thinking that way was selfish. If Doug Meely was no longer himself, how could I still be Patty Meely?

It did not bear thinking about.

So the worry was there: Could Dad perhaps be hiding at Rye Springs? He always called it his hideaway. Could he have managed to get there without being captured? And if he *had* made it to Rye Springs, would he expect me to be there as well?

How could he be sure that I would not have told the FBI all about Rye Springs? Could it be that he trusted me that much? Trust? Amid all of these lies?

I frowned to myself, lying flat on the bed and reaching down to pet the cat as he slept on the floor. A new thought had occurred to me — an extension of an old thought. Assuming that everything I had been told about Dad was the real lie — assuming that all of this was some gross case of mistaken identity — he might have taken the opportunity to escape in a frightened attempt to clear his name. That happened all the time in the movies. The cops would be railroading an innocent man to jail; the man would escape and uncover the true criminal and then be allowed to go free and live his life in peace.

It was almost too much to wish for. . . . Then a more cynical thought hit me. If Dad really was Casper Pelling, he would be long gone by now and would certainly give no thought to some strange rendezvous at Rye Springs. If he were Doug Meely, he would know that his daughter would be smart enough not to come.

None of this explained how I found myself crawling, once again, quietly out of the bedroom window.

I took the jacket they had returned to me and stuffed my pockets with everything I could carry, including my diary. I fell into the hedge, jabbing myself again with the needles. Sneaking out of the yard, I brushed the dirt and green needles from my jeans and jacket. I turned at the corner as I had the night before, but this time I heard a motor quietly starting behind me.

I took my breath in short gasps but managed to not turn back and look.

Wonderful.

I may have been paranoid, but if so it was doing me absolutely no good. I was getting paranoid far too late. I should have suspected, and I was kicking myself for not having thought about it. Would not the daughter of an escaped convict be placed under some sort of surveillance?

Of course she would.

I continued down the street in the direction of the gas station, where I had made the telephone call the night before. Obviously I could not go to Rye Springs.

Unless, it occurred to me, I could manage to shake the tail.

Shake the tail? I almost giggled from the sheer nervous weirdness of it all. My life was definitely becoming like an episode of a television show. And not a very good television show at that.

It was taking everything in me not to turn around and scream back at them. The street was dark, but the car behind me had its headlights on. Maybe they saw no reason to hide their presence.

I turned down a side street and tried to make it look as if that had been my intended path all along. The headlights fell back a little, but they were definitely following.

Another side street. I circled the block. Still the headlights followed.

Wonderful again. I considered heading back to the Gizzales' and going to bed. It wouldn't matter, I supposed. The tails would still report my late-night stroll. I could have tried calling Kimmers again, but the thought made my stomach twist and turn. Instead, I continued walking toward the gas station for no particular reason.

As I got within a block or so, though, I hesitated and started to turn around. Sitting in the gas station lot, drinking beer and making a bit of noise, were four big men on heavy-looking motorcycles. Some sort of biker club, with jackets and riding boots. One of them was speaking to the others, loudly. He was smoking a fat cigar, and its glow flickered in the dark.

I was instinctively retreating when an idea dawned on me. I shivered. If it worked, I would be set, but if it didn't work . . .

I got up my nerve and continued.

As I got closer they stopped talking and started watching me. I knew that at any moment they would make a remark or two, so I surprised them and spoke first. I increased my pace and stepped quickly over to where the motorcycles were parked. "Hey! Could you guys help me?"

The big man with the cigar hunched forward. He was the only one actually sitting on his motorcycle; the others were leaning back against theirs. The big man pushed back the bill of his cap and smirked. "What's bothering you, missy?"

I looked behind me. "You see that car back there? Following me?"

They did. "What about it?"

"There are some men inside. I think they're perverts or something. They tried to get me into their car."

"Oh, yeah?"

"I'm just trying to get home, but now they're following me. I'm scared."

The big biker flicked his stubby cigar away and said, "You don't have to be scared." He started his motorcycle with a kick. "We'll take care of those guys."

I shivered once more for show, but I was actually more than a little proud of myself. Despite several auditions I had never had a part in a school play, but the bikers believed, and now they were tossing their beer cans aside and getting excited at the thought of a little late-night justice. I almost felt sorry for whoever it was following me. Almost. The bikers roared out of the gas station toward the tailing car.

I braced and then ran across the street and down an alley.

My shoes slipped and slid on the gravel, but I pushed myself and ran a little faster. I cut right at the first opportunity and left at the next. I ran, pushing myself, and made turns wherever possible. I was on a side street again, but I kept running. My lungs were burning and my legs were beginning to feel like rubber, but I pushed on.

The more distance between me and my followers the less chance they would find me once they untangled themselves from the bikers. I crossed a few more streets, and when I could run no more, I walked, ducking into hedges and behind trees whenever headlights appeared. I suddenly felt very cold, so I buttoned my jacket tight and continued on.

I did not have a watch, but I figured it had to be nearly midnight. There was no moon.

Walking to Rye Springs was impossible, of course. It would have taken forever, since the FBI had been nice enough to drag me all the way to South Bend, which placed me who knew how far from the lakefront. Lake Michigan. The Indiana Dunes. Rye Springs. Now that I was actually determined to head out, it seemed an impossible objective.

I actually found myself hitchhiking. My first ride was a woman who had been drinking. She smelled like beer and told me she was headed for Terre Haute but would take me at least as far as Interstate 20. I thanked her and buckled my seat belt. She laughed. "You won't need that."

I smiled weakly as she pulled away from the curb at top speed. It was a scary ride, and I was thankful she was not headed west, even if it did mean I would end up walking. She talked a lot about my being careful with men who would want to pick me up for more than just a ride. I nodded but did not say much.

The woman did as she promised and dropped me off by an exit ramp on Interstate 20. I thanked her again, she peeled off, and I started walking. It was very dark, except for the headlights that screeched by me, and I had no idea what time it was anymore. All I knew was that away from the warmth of the woman's car it was very, very cold.

I was nervous every time I stuck out my thumb, but I got lucky and avoided being picked up by any weird types. Instead a large semi-tractor trailer geared down and stopped just ahead of me. The rear of the trailer was a mass of license plates from different states, and I ran up to where the passenger door of the cab was being flung open. "How far are you walking?" a voice asked.

I crawled up and peered inside. "Indiana Dunes."

"This late?" The driver was an extremely thin man who was frowning at me. Soft country and western music played over the static of a citizens band radio and warm air rushed out of his cab.

"It's a school project. A beach camp-out. I missed the bus."

I could see immediately that he did not believe me — it was a really stupid story — but all he said was "Climb on in before you let all the warm out." I did, and he shifted back into gear and pulled away from the shoulder. I expected him to be talkative like the drunk woman, but he never really said anything to me. I guess he was afraid I would think he was coming on to me or something. He changed tapes a couple of times — it was the same kind of music Dad listened to — and he sang along to some of the songs.

"You have to be real careful out there tonight," he said finally.

"What?" I guess I was falling asleep in the comfortable warmth of the cab.

"You have to be careful. I don't know where you're really going this morning, but you have to be especially careful. There's a bad man out there."

Jolted, I felt wide awake again. "Who?"

"Spy. Broke out of prison some years back, I guess. It was on the radio. They caught him, but he escaped again this morning. Somewhere along the Interstate."

"Is . . . is he dangerous?"

"Radio said he was."

I didn't say anything else about it.

Finally we passed an exit sign that said INDIANA DUNES ¾ MILE. He creaked the truck along the shoulder and stopped. "This is as far as I can get you."

"I know," I said. "Thanks."

I climbed down from the cab, slamming the door shut behind me. The air brakes hissed and the truck pulled away, wobbling a bit. A milk truck. That was the only time I noticed. MASSON DAIRY was printed on the side of the trailer. I watched as the red and white lights disappeared over the next hill, and then I started up the road toward the dunes.

I guess it was about three or four in the morning. I half expected some drug-crazed maniac to come charging out at me from the shadows. My heart was pounding. There were stories like that all the time: TEENAGE GIRL FOUND RAPED AND STABBED TO DEATH ON LAKEFRONT. Shallow graves and all that terrible stuff. I shivered and plodded on, reaching the first of the dunes and shuffling through the sand.

There was more light at the top of the dune. Even without a moon some sort of light seemed to be reflecting off the lake. I don't know where the light came from — maybe it was a great reflection of the city lights. All I do know is that the lake seemed as vast and endless as an ocean, and in a way that was comforting. I listened to the water slap the beach for a while, and then I continued on.

Rye Springs was not all that much farther once I figured out where I was, but I cut my right hand as I tried to slide down into the little hidden cove. Some sort of sharp rock hidden under the sand. It was not as light here because the dune blocked out the lake. There were a few trees, some waist-high beach grass, and a small pond, spring-fed, which snaked tightly between two dunes to reach the lake.

The water looked cold, and I was thinking that the truth — so far as I would ever understand it — was obvious. My father was a stranger to me. Best forgotten. And this stranger was probably making his way to either Canada or Mexico.

I felt it as a weight, but I didn't know whether that weight was falling on me or being lifted from my shoulders. I suppose in a way I was relieved. I wished him nothing but luck, although luck seemed to be the one thing he did not need. His successful jailbreak had made "the Pelling Luck" a popular topic in the newspapers.

I stood beside that pool of water and tried to ignore the warm trickles down my cheeks.

Alone again, I thought. Just like the song said.

Until a firm and familiar voice behind me said, "Hello, Patty."

SIX

We were driving. The car was a new brown station wagon which Dad had parked in one of the empty beach parking lots about a half mile from Rye Springs. We were headed west and the sun was just peeking up behind us.

I finally asked. "Where did you get the car?"

Dad never looked away from the road. "I took it."

"What?"

"Relax. I took a brand-new car because the owners will absolutely have it insured. The insurance company will replace it, and the only ones who will be out any money will be some faceless conglomerate."

My mind was going crazy. I have to admit that after I was startled by Dad's voice at Rye Springs, my initial emotion had been overwhelming relief. I actually grabbed him tight and cried in his arms. Despite everything that had happened I felt safe there. From that first moment, though, I saw that he was not the same. Outwardly, anyway.

His hair was short and had been bleached a stark blond. He was wearing a red checkered flannel shirt and baggy blue slacks with tennis shoes. In that first instant I had turned to the voice but not recognized him. Then he stepped closer and I saw his face. It was Dad. He led me quickly from Rye Springs down the beach to the lot and the waiting car.

Now the only way I could keep myself from babbling and shrieking was to begin sorting through the glove compartment. It was full of papers: white papers, yellow papers, blue papers. All with someone else's name written on them.

"Aren't the cops going to be after this car?"

"Not right away. I switched license plates with another car. By the time they sort all that out, we'll be where we're going."

"Where are we going?"

"Away."

When I had first climbed into the car I was still too swept up by seeing Dad and being warmed from the heater to ask any questions. I felt comfortable there and even fell asleep for a while. Now I was awake again and scared. I was scared because the questions I thought I had to ask were almost as frightening as the answers.

"Where did you get those clothes?"

He didn't answer at first, but then he said, "They came with the car."

My lip quivered again. I bit down on it. My lips

were getting totally out of control and I didn't like that.

Dad looked over at me. "As soon as possible we have to make a stop. Maybe in Bloomington."

"Bloomington?"

"Bloomington, Illinois."

I looked around. The sunrise was in its red stage and cast weird colors on the surrounding wheat and corn fields. "Where are we now?"

"South of Kankakee still headed west. Only difference is now we're on Route 24."

"When did we get off the Interstate?"

"While you were asleep. We're better off on the side roads."

I did not ask why.

Dad looked over at me, obviously embarrassed. "I'm sorry, baby. But when we stop in Bloomington we need to get your hair cut. Maybe even dyed."

I did not let that shock me. Instead I asked a question. "Are we running now?"

He nodded. "I'm afraid we are."

So on we drove. The only other comment Dad made was a general one. "I knew that you would be there," he said. "You were always smart and quick."

"I was scared."

"Yeah. I guess you were."

"Can I turn on the radio?"

Dad looked at me again. "Will it upset you?"

I frowned. "What?"

"Never mind."

I reached down and switched it on. Music played for a while and then it was time for the news. The top story was the near crash of a jumbo jet carrying 277 people to Japan. One engine had exploded south of Tokyo, but the pilot managed to land without injuries. The second story began. "*Fugitive Casper Pelling is still at large, following a second spectacular escape from federal authorities. Pelling, who was arrested Friday, nearly twenty years after his original escape from a federal penitentiary in California —*"

I looked at Dad. He kept his eyes tight on the road.

"*— is believed to have been working in an Indiana steel mill at the time of his arrest. He is reportedly accompanied by his fifteen-year-old daughter, Patricia —*"

Oh, my God.

"*— whom he fathered with an unknown woman now believed deceased. Pelling, convicted of espionage in 1965, is described as six feet one inch tall with light brown hair and no distinguishing features.*"

I looked at Dad. No distinguishing features?

"*Patricia Pelling is described as approximately five feet three inches tall, one hundred two pounds —*"

How much?

"*— with shoulder-length blond hair. Pelling is considered dangerous. Anyone who may have information as to his whereabouts is asked to contact —*"

I switched off the radio and hunched down in the seat, trying to push myself deep into the upholstery. Dad still kept his eyes tight on the road.

"Did you do it?"

He blinked. "What?"

"Did you do what they said you did?"

"What? Escape?"

"All of it."

He cocked an eye toward me. It was a strange and cold gesture and I shivered inside again. "Okay," he said. "Storytime. Ready?"

I did my best to nod.

"A long time ago, when the world and I were younger, I did some things. Maybe they were right, maybe they were wrong. Maybe they just were."

"What did you do?"

"I . . . I took some pictures and diagrams and gave them to a man. That man gave me money, and that money helped make life happen."

I was looking at Dad, and he turned from the road to look at me.

"Patty, I didn't even know the man's name. I thought he was from Rockwell or Boeing or one of JTR's other competitors. I didn't know he was a Russian or KGB or whoever he was supposed to be. He was just a man with some money."

I thought about that. Traffic was becoming heavier, so I hunched down further to avoid being seen. "Would you have sold him the papers if you had known that he was Russian?"

Dad was quiet now. It was starting to sprinkle and he switched on the windshield wipers. "What would you like me to say, Patty? No? I would like very much to say no — an honest no — but I'm no longer sure. Right now, from inside this fish bowl, they all look alike to me. American, Russian, Chinese. So maybe twenty years ago I wouldn't have sold the papers to a Russian, but today I think maybe I would."

In the oncoming lane was an Illinois state trooper. He passed us without so much as a glance. I nearly fainted. Dad laughed, a deep genuine laugh. "Relax."

"How can I relax?"

He shook his head and smiled. "Stop worrying about the police. I avoided them for twenty years. Don't you think I can avoid them for another twenty?"

"But —"

"I'm more worried about all this publicity." He switched the radio back on. "See if you can find some country music, will you?"

I started scanning the dial. "Why are you worried so much about the publicity?"

"I'm worried about some people who are just a little smarter than the police sometimes. Bad people."

That gave me another chill. I found a station that had a twanging steel guitar and turned the volume up a bit. "What people?"

Dad looked over at me. "Sit up. You don't need to crouch like that. It's bad for your posture."

I sat up, but I didn't feel very good about it. "What people?" I asked again.

"CIA. Or CISNA. Or NSA. Whatever you want to call them: spooks, spies, sleepers. I had them thinking I had gone to Russia, and that was fine. Only now they know different. They are sitting around telephones waiting patiently for a call from someone saying, 'Yeah, he's in town here. At a hotel.' That's why I had to get away from the police again, Patty. These are terrible people I'm talking about. You have to believe that."

I nodded. "I believe you." But I don't know if I really did.

Dad looked at me again. "If these people find me, they won't bother to arrest me. They will kill me, on the spot. I don't want you to be around if that happens."

"Is . . . is it going to happen?"

Dad smiled then. "Of course not. As long as you're with me you'll know I feel safe."

But I didn't feel safe.

Shortly after ten o'clock that Sunday morning we passed a sign which read ENTERING BLOOMINGTON, ILLINOIS — HOME OF ILLINOIS STATE UNIVERSITY. MAYOR GLYNNIS WAGNER WELCOMES YOU.

"We have to get some gas," Dad said. "Then we'll see if we can find a place to get your hair done, and then we'll find a motel."

"All of those things cost money," I said.

"Yes."

"So where are we getting it?"

"It came with the car and the clothes."

That *really* bothered me.

Dad coasted us into an Exxon station. We had just entered the city proper, and shops and businesses cluttered the area, but most seemed closed. The bells pinged inside the service station as Dad stopped. A short man with a wild grin and wire-framed glasses stepped into the doorway. "It's self-service!"

Dad rolled down the window. "What's that?"

"Self-service. You pump the gas yourself."

Dad nodded and popped open the door. We had driven past the actual rain, but the sky was still overcast. "I'm going to the bathroom," I said as I got out of the car.

Dad nodded and pulled the cap off the gas tank. He reached for the pump.

I started to walk around the corner of the station but the man said, "If you're going to the ladies' room you need the key."

I followed him into the station. Beside the register were two keys, each connected to a large piece of wood on which was burned MEN'S and WOMEN'S. I took the key and went around the side of the station. When I returned the key the man said, "You're all from Indiana?"

"Yeah. So?"

"So nothing. I just like to read license plates. Not that much else to do here since we went self-service."

"When did you go self-service?"

"Twenty minutes ago when the boss took off for the day." The man laughed as if he had just said the funniest thing ever. I went back outside. "Watch out for that guy."

Dad was recapping the gas tank. "Why?"

"All his lights are on but there's nobody home."

Dad nodded and went inside to pay for the gas, and I sat in the car thinking almost normal thoughts about Bloomington. I was wondering about breakfast a lot, too. It's amazing how fast your mind accepts the wildest and most terrible situations and starts wondering "Does this town have a McDonald's?" or "Do the motels have a movie channel?"

Dad came out and we drove deeper into town. For a few moments I was able to pretend that everything that had happened in the last few days was a bad dream. All the familiar franchise names were there. We passed a movie theater: CINEMA I*II*III. It was almost possible for me to believe that Dad was just taking me to a new shopping mall. He was bringing me here to find something for my birthday.

He reached in his pocket as he drove and produced a pack of cigarettes and a lighter. He pulled one from the pack and placed it between his lips, lighting it.

I looked at him. "You don't smoke."

"I do now."

"Did those come with the car too?"

He took a deep drag, exhaled, then looked at me. "No. I bought them at the gas station."

I looked out my window again.

Dad asked, "Are you hungry?"

"Very."

"I'll stop at a supermarket."

Which he did. He returned with a bag from which he produced two small containers of milk, a box of

90

doughnuts, and a newspaper. It was the *Bloomington Express Daily*, the thick Sunday edition. "Do you want the funnies?" he asked.

I meant to say no but instead nodded and took the section. Dad quickly scanned the front pages. I munched a doughnut and tore open my milk, trying to drink without letting it dribble down my chin. My teeth were wearing their wool sweaters again, and I felt dirty and tired. I forced myself to read every comic in the section, including the soap opera cartoons that I never looked at. Dad finished the article he had been engrossed in and started flipping idly through the rest of the paper.

"How bad is it?" I asked.

He shrugged. "Bad enough, I guess. But just wait. Tomorrow after we get some rest I'll show you a few tricks." He folded the paper and flipped it across the seat into the back. Without even bothering to eat a doughnut or touch his milk, he started the car again.

As unlikely as I thought the possibility was, we did find an open hair salon. Arrowshaw Hair Stylists. We barely made it, rolling into the parking lot at twenty minutes before twelve. The sign on the door said the salon closed at noon. It also said NO APPOINTMENT NECESSARY! WALK RIGHT IN!

I looked at Dad. "How should I get it cut?"

"Different."

"Anything special?"

"Just make it different."

He fished into his pocket and came out with some

bills and peeled off a twenty for me. Where was he getting all this money? *A rough character,* I remembered Marshal Mitch saying. *A genuine nasty.* But those were my words; Marshal Mitch only stole them from my diary to lay them on my dad.

I pushed open the glass door of the salon and sat down. A woman with a stack of red hair atop her head smiled and said she would be with me in two shakes of a lamb's tail.

I was remembering things now. Or maybe I was just so tired that I was beginning to dream while I was awake.

I remembered how Mark used to talk about my hair, how he used to tell me how pretty it was. Larry used to say things like that too, but not as often, and for some reason it never meant as much coming from him. I always complained that neither one of them had to wash it. That was a task and a half, washing that hair. I used to wear it midway down my back, — the grand accumulation of fifteen years of uncut growth — but last summer I gave up and had it trimmed to my shoulders. From the looks I got from everyone, you might have thought I dyed it green. I had even been thinking about getting a permanent wave.

Now, faced with the prospect of actually having my head so abruptly altered, I felt genuinely upset. I was worried that I might step outside the salon as someone else. I read somewhere that a hair style can totally change your personality and I guess that has

92

to be at least sort of true: I did not feel like the same person I was at fourteen with long hair.

I knew that when I got my hair slashed this time I was going to become somebody entirely unknown to me, maybe even somebody who I would not like very much.

And there was absolutely no going back.

SEVEN

A sleep without dreams is not nearly as restful as you might think, and I awoke groggy and tired in our motel room. I reached up and clicked on the light. It was still the same small, clean room of the Golden Key Roadside Inn.

Terrific.

The other double bed in the room was empty, and the bedspread was lying half on the floor. The chain was off the door, so I knew right away that Dad was gone. Where? No thoughts came to mind. I didn't even know if it was night or day; there was no clock in the room and the curtains were drawn. I lifted the telephone.

"Check-out."

"Wha . . . what time is it?"

"Just about nine-twenty."

"At night?"

The voice smirked. "Nine-twenty in the morning, miss."

"Just testing." I hung up the phone and dragged myself over the side of the bed to the floor. I didn't have a change of clothes, so I was still wearing my blue blouse. I slipped my jeans on and walked barefoot into the bathroom. The air in the room smelled artificial. No, that's not right. The air smelled, if you can believe this, rented. Just like the beds and the TV and the shower, the air was rented. Wonderful. I looked around the bathroom, and since I could not find a complimentary toothbrush or toothpaste, I had to wash my mouth out with cool water again. My teeth were going to wind up rotting right out of my head, not to mention what was happening to my breath.

I was leaving the bathroom when I suddenly realized the difference the haircut had made in my appearance. Dad had been pleased with the change, but I guess I was too numbed by everything to notice myself. Now it gave me a start. It wasn't me at all.

Well, it was me but it wasn't *me*. My hair, which used to be held down by its weight, was curling right back up and frizzing out. To tell the truth, it looked wild. Bouncy. For a minute I regretted not having any make-up to cover my freckles with. My nose has always been too thin and pointed, but now I realized that my new look made my cheekbones look higher. Classic cheekbones of a fashion model. Putting my hands in my hair, I almost giggled. It might have been the pressure of the whole situation, but I was really happy with the way it had turned out. I should have cut it sooner. It definitely made me look older, maybe even sexier. Who knows?

I let my hands drop and went back to the room. I tried to peek out through the curtains without actually opening them. It was a clear morning and the sun was showing itself proud. Even the clouds looked content. The station wagon wasn't where Dad had parked it the night before. He was definitely gone.

Where?

Had he left me?

Why was I getting so accustomed to all of this strangeness? Shouldn't I be hysterical? I wondered.

I turned from the window and switched the television on. My stomach growled. Why was I always hungry these days? If this kept up I was going to wind up grotesquely fat. Fat, dirty, and all of my teeth gone. I flipped the TV dial around once. There were twenty-two cable stations — mostly cartoon shows, exercise shows, game shows, and public service programs. I left it on one called *Good Morning, Bloomington!* and turned the sound up.

I held my breath for nearly twenty minutes, but they never mentioned Dad or me. It was local news — stories about donations to the public library and a home for stray cats. Finally the host blinded the camera with his teeth and said goodbye. I flipped to a game show. *Hollywood Squares.*

Keys jingled in the door. I snapped stiff on the edge of the bed, my heart pounding. The door creaked open: It was Dad.

I blew out air. "Hey!"

"Good morning."

He shut the door. He was wearing a black lightweight jacket which I didn't ask about; instead I said, "Where were you?"

"I had to get rid of the car. No sense taking risks. Also I had a few things to do before you woke up."

"Did you sleep at all?"

"Yeah. Sure I did."

I thought a minute. "Hey, if you got rid of the car, how are we going to get around?"

"I have that covered. We have a replacement vehicle," he said.

"You stole it?"

"I prefer to call it recently obtained."

I looked at Dad like he was some alien from a science-fiction movie. Casually obtained automobiles? Mysterious money? Clothes that appeared by magic? The answers to my questions did not require much imagination, and that was what really scared me.

"Are you going to keep stealing cars?"

He shook his head. "I knew you wouldn't like that. The car is just for this morning. This afternoon we board the *Western Flyer*."

"The what?"

"It's a train. I bet you didn't even know Bloomington had an Amtrak station."

"There are a lot of things I didn't know."

Dad paused, looking as though I had slapped him across the face. He recovered quickly, saying, "We didn't stay over here last night by accident. There is a plan."

"What is it?"

He just smiled.

"Where are we going?"

"California."

"Why California?"

"Why not? Don't you like California?"

"Won't they be looking for you there?"

"They are looking for me everywhere. California is just the first stop."

"This plan sounds complicated."

"At first, yes. It will grow on you."

I took an unnecessary breath and asked, "How long can we get away with all of this?"

He frowned.

"We can't just live this lie."

"Patty, you are going to be surprised at exactly what you will do to keep on living. Lie or no lie."

I waited. "Does that include murder?"

Dad had been walking into the bathroom but he froze. Turned. "What?"

"Would you kill someone to stay out of jail?"

"What kind of a question is that?"

"I don't know. Have you got an answer to it?"

"I hope it never comes down to that."

"But what if it does?"

"Patty, what do you want me to say?"

"I want you to say no."

"Patty . . ." He let out a sigh. "I'm not going to start lying to you now. . . ."

"What?" I couldn't help raising my voice, which was something I had done with my father maybe once or twice before in my entire life. What he had said totally shocked me. It seemed like such a really stupid statement to make, considering the circumstances. "Dad, when are you going to *stop* lying to me?"

"What?"

"Everything you ever told me in my *entire life* was a lie."

"That's not true."

"No? Where are we now, Dad? On vacation?"

"Patty, what do you want me to say?"

I was crying now, breaking down. "I want you to say that none of this is true. Say it's all a bad dream. Make it go away, Daddy, please make it go away!"

I was blubbering.

He stepped forward and took me into his arms. But he couldn't stop me from crying, no matter how many words of comfort he gave me. My eyes were closed, and I was realizing — maybe for the first time or maybe for the third or fourth — that my dad was still back at Kreuger High, waiting for me in the car. Doug Meely was gone. Casper Pelling was the name of the man I was with. He was wearing my dad's face and seemed to be having no trouble with his voice, but I guess my dad's memories didn't fit quite right with him. Casper Pelling was not my dad. He could not be. He was a stranger.

I cried for I don't know exactly how long until finally I pulled away. I went into the bathroom and wiped my eyes with a cold, wet washcloth. The cool water stung against my hot face. I sniffed, blew my nose, and then washed my face again. Finally I was ready to face the world. Dad was watching *Name That Tune* and acting as if nothing had happened.

"So where did you go this morning?"

He didn't look over. The lady on television was trying to identify a song from *The Sound of Music* in less than five notes. "I made a few stops. You'll see. Go ahead and get your shoes on. We need to check out of this rat trap."

I sat down on the bed and started to pull on my socks. "Where are we going?"

"To the library."

I nodded, thinking he was kidding, but after I got my shoes on we really did check out and go to the library. The Bloomington Municipal Public Library. We drove over in a new green Chevy Impala which, I noticed, had Illinois license plates. There were no keys in the ignition. There was, in fact, no ignition.

"How did you do that?" I asked.

Dad frowned and shrugged. "Wasn't hard. You know how turning a key clicks the ignition system? I've bypassed all that by removing the keylock setup. All I have to do now is touch two wires together."

"Where did you learn that?"

"Trade school."

"Where?"

Dad looked me in the eye. "In prison, Patty. I learned to steal cars in prison."

I found I couldn't hold his gaze.

We parked the car and walked up the library steps. Dad led me toward the back. We looked around the stacks until we found the photocopy machine. "Every library has a copying machine," said Dad. He fished some coins out of his pocket and produced a blue paper which he unfolded. It was a birth certificate.

"Where did you get that?"

"That's a secret. I'm going to show you a little trick." Dad placed the certificate on the copier and made two copies. Then he refolded the original, slid it into his jacket pocket, and grabbed the copies. "Come on. There's one other thing a library always has lying around. A typewriter."

He was right. A young librarian pointed one out for us on the second floor. Nobody else was using it so Dad sat himself in the seat and I looked over his shoulder. From his jacket pocket he produced a small bottle. "This covers typing mistakes," he said. He used the correction fluid to blot out the names and dates on both copies of the birth certificate. He left all the other information: the hospital, doctor, and state.

After the pages had dried, Dad rolled the first certificate into the typewriter. He looked around. There was no one within earshot.

"What do you want to be called?" he asked.

"What?"

"I'm changing your name."

I didn't know what to say.

"How about Karen?"

I didn't say anything. I just watched as he typed a new name over the one that had been whited out.

"What about a middle name?"

I was watching what he had done, and I couldn't help taking shorter breaths. I was becoming a new person. "Millicent," I said.

KAREN MILLICENT PETERSON.

"We'll keep your birthday so you won't be confused," he said. He typed APRIL 4, and then the year.

"You got the year wrong," I said.

Dad shook his head. "I made you two years older so we can get you a driver's license."

That felt good. Older. A driver's license. I got a little excited about the whole thing. "Hey, how come this is so easy?"

Dad shrugged, pulling the paper from the typewriter. "It's not, really. This isn't the best way, but for now it'll have to do. After we get settled I can get us certified copies, anything we need. We'll get by well enough until then, though. It's a paper jungle out there. No one computer can keep track of it all, so they have to use a lot of different computers. And wherever one computer stops and another begins, there is a gap. We are going to live in those gaps."

He rolled in the second copy and typed LOUIS ARTHUR PETERSON.

"I always wanted to be called Lou," he explained.

I watched as he typed in new dates, keeping his own birthdate and year. "Is this what you did before?"

Dad sort of sighed. "Yeah."

"Is that really your birthday?"

He pulled the paper from the typewriter and smiled. "You know something? I really don't remember."

"I can see one problem," I said.

"Which is?" He blinked.

"Isn't it sort of a coincidence that Lou and Karen Peterson were born in the same hospital, with the same doctor and the same parents?" I pointed to the information that hadn't been changed on either form.

Dad smiled kind of sheepishly, the same smile he used to give me when I caught him putting a stuffed animal or some silly toy in my room. He said, "I guess we'll just have to be careful about anyone seeing them both at the same time."

We took the forgeries back down to the copy machine and copied them once more. The new copies looked perfect — as if Karen Millicent Peterson and Louis Arthur Peterson had taken their birth certificates down to the library to make copies of them. Dad ripped the originals into little pieces and threw them in the trash can beside the machine. He folded our new birth certificates and put them in his jacket pocket.

Then he took me shopping.

Bloomington has a small shopping mall which we located with little difficulty. Dad seemed to have this endless supply of money, and he surprised me even more by producing a credit card in one store. I couldn't watch and turned away, terrified, to look at the color televisions on display. The news was on, and I saw myself staring back from the screen. My picture was displayed next to Dad's behind a commentator whom I couldn't hear because the volume on all the sets was turned down. I nearly had heart failure right then and there until I realized that Dad and I no longer looked like the photos. It didn't make me feel much better, but it did keep me from dying of terminal fear.

We bought all the things Dad said we would need for the trip: toothbrushes, toothpaste, soap, shampoo, towels. Dad didn't pick up any shaving items, and I mentioned it: He was showing quite a dark stubble.

He shook his head. "I'm letting it grow." Instead he got a small bottle of peroxide bleach and some cotton balls. He held them up and asked me, "What do you think? Is it true blonds have more fun?"

I had to laugh.

The pressure seemed to be lifting some. We stopped at Penney's for underwear, socks, and two changes of clothes for each of us. "Look around — find what you want," he said. I hesitated, seeing the expanse of the store before me. It felt weird — I wanted to shop, but it didn't seem right.

Dad nodded, understanding. "Don't worry about it, honey. Remember when I took you to the Scottsdale Mall? And I started telling you about *Someday*?"

I nodded. I felt scared for a minute and grabbed Dad's hand. He squeezed and I said, remembering: "*Someday* we'll be able to get anything we want."

Dad smiled. "Surprise."

"What?"

"It's *Someday*."

That was all I needed to hear. Dad pulled two fifty-dollar bills from his wallet, and then two more. He handed all four to me. The money felt dry and crisp, not even real, but I could tell it was. I wanted to hand it back, to say I wanted no part of it. After all, where was it coming from? But at the same time I felt the excitement starting all over again. Why shouldn't it be *someday*? Hadn't Dad and I been through enough to deserve a *someday*?

I had a fantastic afternoon.

It was a day I never knew before. Was this the way rich people lived? I felt wicked but not guilty. I loved it! I bought myself a pair of jeans and some black brushed cords. A black lace shirtdress looked beautiful on me, so I grabbed it, too. Considering my new, older look, I got myself a leotard to go with the sweatshirt I rang up as well. I also found myself a belt and, when Dad suggested it, a new pair of shoes. I hate to say it, but I wound up asking Dad for more money.

At first our things were in four sacks, but Dad

bought a couple of airline carry-on bags, and that made us more organized. I was still high on the excitement of it all when we stopped at the Orange Julius: I had a chili dog and Dad ordered one smothered in relish and ketchup. That was the way he always ate hot dogs. I was starting to recover: I was traveling with Dad, not some stranger named Pelling. After lunch we played video games for a while. I beat him at four straight tangles on SpaceKite, but he still trounced me on Gunfight at the OK Corral. Dad always won that one. He made me laugh again by slipping into a music store and coming out wearing headphones and carrying one of those tiny cassette players. He was dancing a bit and popping his fingers like it was hard and fast music. I took a listen and groaned: country and western. When he handed it over, though, he gave me three more tapes, and one of them was the new Walrus release, the one Kimmers had just got.

Kimmers. Bam. Back in the real world again.

I guess I got a little quieter then and Dad noticed. "We should probably get mobile," he said. I just nodded, pulling the strap of my bag up onto my shoulder. Looking for the exit closest to the car took a few minutes, and it was almost four-thirty when we stepped outside the mall. Dad produced a pair of aviator sunglasses and ripped the price tag off before slipping them on. We were crossing the parking lot when he abruptly slowed his pace. "Hold up a little."

I looked over, confused, still caught up in everything and still thinking about Kimmers. "What?"

"Don't panic. Just turn around like we forgot something."

"What?" But by then, of course, I saw what Dad had already seen. Near our green Chevy, red lights were flashing. A Bloomington police cruiser.

One cop was walking slowly around the car, inspecting it. A second was sitting on the passenger side of the patrol car with the door open, speaking into a radio.

I shuddered. "Oh, my God."

"Relax." Dad spoke low and soothing.

"But —"

"We forgot something, Karen."

"What?"

"Don't forget your name now, *Karen*." He emphasized it for me. "Just stay cool."

"Oh, God."

"Let's head back for the mall." Dad touched me lightly on the arm and turned me. I saw his eyes then: They were ice. I was terrified, absolutely positive that we were both going to be caught and taken to jail, but he was totally calm. We moved back across the lot and into the mall again.

Despite the time of year, the mall was running its air conditioning. I hadn't really noticed it before, but now I was shivering. "What are we going to do?"

"Nothing. We're not going to do anything."

"But what about the car?"

"Did you leave anything in it? Anything? Think!"

"No, I didn't. I didn't have anything to leave."

"Okay, then."

We walked through one corridor. At the end was a large buffalo statue I had admired earlier in the day. The statue was outside a china store, and I thought it was great — I love stuff like that. Cigar-store Indians, the huge concrete chickens they put in front of some fast-food places, wooden decoy ducks. I can't explain why, but I think weird things like that are really great.

I wasn't charmed by the buffalo this time, though. I was too terrified. Dad seemed distracted. He was muttering to himself. "Careless, careless . . ."

"What is it?" I felt my heart was going to pound right through my chest.

"Listen to me. I want you to go look in Carsons' for a while. Fifteen minutes. Then meet me in front of the mall, near the taxi stand."

"Why can't I just stay with you?"

"I need to check things out."

"But —"

"Just go!"

I made an abrupt twist on my heels, and walked away from dad on what Mrs. Zachs would have called a perfect ninety-degree angle. What the real angle was I couldn't say.

Dad wanted me to go to Carsons', and since it was the nearest store I did. I was literally shaking as I

108

walked the aisles. What was happening? Was it ending here? I had a very scary, very selfish thought: What would happen to *me*? I felt sick for even thinking it, but until now I had claimed total innocence. I hadn't known anything. Now I was involved and, as the clothes stuffed in my bag showed, obviously enjoying it.

What was happening to me?

I looked toward the clock at the far end of the store. Twelve minutes more and I was supposed to be out front, by the taxi stand. Where would we go next? How long could we run?

My hands were shaking.

I stopped at the cosmetics and aimlessly pushed around the bottles. Perfumes, colognes, lotions. I tried to keep my hands from shaking. Come on, I thought. If you're so smart, what do you do now?

"Can I help you with something?" a man's voice said.

I jumped, startled, and started to say, "No, I was just —"

It was Helker.

EIGHT

Special Agent Robert Helker, my old FBI buddy from South Bend, standing beside me in the Bloomington, Illinois, Carsons' cosmetics department. And he was smiling.

So it was ending here.

I was at the bottom of a pool, fighting to reach the air above. I was caught in a deep dream, unable to escape. It was a nightmare, the worst ever, and standing before me was a genuine nasty, the one who wouldn't let me wake up. And he was smiling.

So it was ending here.

As always, Helker couldn't help but twitch as he smiled. It was so false an expression on him. He gestured at the bottles. "Have you found something you like? Perhaps we can purchase one for the road. I'm sure they all smell very exciting on you, Miss Pelling. Oh, and I see that you've changed your hair. It's very attractive."

I didn't say anything.

"Your friend Walt Rogers will be so disappointed. You know, you had him totally convinced you didn't know anything at all. Totally convinced. You're very good."

"I —"

"Save it."

I felt numbed. Helker was a horrible vision I was trying to blink away. He said, "Could you excuse me just a minute?" Still the phony smile. He lifted one of the walkie-talkies I had first seen that terrible afternoon (only days ago?), when they grabbed Dad at school.

So it was ending here.

Where was Dad? Did they have him already?

Helker was speaking into his radio. "Cobra? This is Viper. Come in."

Static.

His radio cackled and spat back at him. He frowned and tried again. "Cobra, this is Viper. Come in."

Still static. Popping and cracking noises, but no answer.

Helker muttered some profanity. He tried a third time, still with no success. He looked around the store, then nodded knowingly. "It's the hair dryers."

I blinked but didn't say anything.

He pointed to a beauty salon in the rear of the store. "The hair dryers back there are jamming the radio. Happens sometimes. Can't get through in here, so I guess we need to step outside. . . ." He started to grab me.

That was when I got him.

When he first spoke, I had my right hand wrapped around an uncapped sample bottle of Chimere perfume. It didn't mean anything until I realized that he couldn't get through to anybody on his radio. There might still be a chance! When Helker tried to pull me away from the counter, I snatched the perfume bottle and gave him three quick squirts in the eyes.

"Hey!" He yelped, stumbling back.

The radio clattered to the aisle floor.

My first instinct was to bolt, but he reached for me blindly, snagging my blouse. He was howling, one hand rubbing furiously at his eyes and the other pulling me. I freaked, too, and clawed at his hand, drawing blood with my nails. He was almost doubled over, and I pushed him back into the display case. He was fumbling now, holding his eyes and hollering. Without thinking, I grabbed his radio and took off with it.

"Hey!" He was yelling. "That girl! God, my eyes! Stop that girl!"

I ran.

I could hear him howling, but he didn't identify himself as a cop or a special agent or anything, and nobody around us knew what was going on, I guess. One guy grabbed me just as I reached the exit, but I screamed, "Where's a phone?" and he reacted on reflex, letting me go and pointing down the corridor.

So I kept running.

I had this sudden image of Helker kneeling like in the movies, pistol drawn, sight fixed square between my shoulder blades. . . . But no shot rang out. He was still out of it.

So I kept running down the mall corridor.

The radio screeched as I ran, and I nearly dropped it. *"Viper, this is Cobra. We're still waiting on those car stats. Are you en route to the mall?"*

I hit the tinted glass mall doors at full speed and didn't even slow down. I had no idea where I was going, but I was definitely going. The glass doors slammed back, and a hand seized my arm. I whirled, swinging the radio like a club, but it was Dad. He looked alarmed. "What? What's wrong?"

"They're here!"

"What?"

I thrust the radio at him. He still didn't understand me, but the radio cackled: *"Viper, this is Cobra. Radio check?"*

His eyes went wide. "Where did you . . ."

I snapped a look behind me, into the mall. Back at where Helker was. I was panting.

Dad didn't finish his question. He realized everything in that instant and grabbed me again. He pulled me past the welcome sign — BLOOMINGTON SPRING-LAND MALL: A FUN PLACE TO BE! — and shoved me toward the cab parked at the taxi stand. There was a lady already sitting in back and it was starting to take off, but Dad leaped off the curb, banging his fist on the door. It jerked to a stop and Dad yanked the door open.

The woman in the back was about forty years old, and her eyes were wide with shock. Dad climbed in beside her, pulling me behind.

The driver looked back over the seat. "Hey, buddy, no way. Out!"

Dad produced a gun.

Not just a gun, like the ones so casually waved on television, but a *gun*: black steel, oily, and very heavy-looking. Dad's hand seemed to heft a weight. He didn't lift it at the driver; he just poked it into the back seat. "No questions. Just drive. Now."

The cabbie went instantly white and said, "I'm driving." He slammed on the gas and we jerked forward again.

Dad looked at the woman. "Are you all right?"

She stammered. "Fine."

"You mind sharing a cab?"

"No, no, of course not. No." She was babbling.

Dad nodded at her, trying to be calm. "Thank you."

Something weird was happening to me. It had started, maybe, with Helker, but it really began when I saw Dad pull the gun. I zapped totally beyond nerves and fear. I felt instantly calm. At peace. It was a freaky feeling.

Helker's radio screeched again: *"Viper, Cobra. Radio check?"*

I snatched it up, pressing the button. "Loud and clear!"

114

Dad grabbed it, switching it off. He looked away from me.

The cabbie took the cab into the flow of traffic, leaving the mall parking lot. He whispered back at me. "Hey, uh, miss . . . are you being kidnapped? Is that it?"

I shook my head. "No. I'm helping kidnap you."

The woman said, "What? Are we being kidnapped?"

Dad had been looking behind us, but now he snapped forward again, sounding annoyed. "Nobody is being kidnapped. Everybody relax. I just needed to get out of there fast and without a discussion."

"You needed to escape from a *shopping mall*?"

"I was in a hurry."

"What? You guys shoplifters?"

"No."

"All you had to do was take the next cab. No problem."

"No time. Start your meter."

The cabbie's hands shook, but he pulled the red flag down and the meter started clicking. It started at three dollars. "This is a fare?"

"This is a fare."

The cabbie nodded. "So where am I going?"

"I don't know. Any suggestions?"

"How about if I take you home?"

"I wish you could. Any other ideas?"

"A hotel maybe?"

Dad shook his head. "Just drive for a while."

The woman cleared her throat and said, "I have to be home soon. My husband —"

Dad cut her off. "This won't take long." He smiled. "I'll pay your cab fare."

She tried to smile back.

Dad looked at me. He had the gun in his right hand and Helker's radio in his left. He seemed to weigh it in his palm. "I'd like to ask about this. . . ."

I shook my head. "Not now."

"Yeah. Not now."

The cabbie asked, "Hey, you always use the hardware?"

"No, not really."

"You running from the cops?"

"No."

"The mob?"

Dad shook his head. "You watch too many movies."

"Yeah, my life should be a movie."

"Maybe it should."

"Hey, look," said the cabbie. "It's all right with me if you feel like putting that thing away. I mean, in case we hit some bumps or anything. I get real nervous."

"Don't be nervous. Nobody gets hurt."

"Is that a promise?"

"That's a promise."

The cabbie spoke to me again. "Does he keep his promises?"

116

"Usually."

Dad put the gun back beneath his coat. Again, the question was, Where did he get it?

The cabbie asked me another question. "You always hang out with hoods?"

"He's not a hood."

"What is he then? CIA? A spy?"

The cabbie was looking at me in the rearview mirror when he asked this, and I saw his eyes change. They went cold with fright. The woman beside us gasped. Dad muttered something, but the cabbie spoke the loudest. "Oh, wow."

I asked, "What does that mean?"

"It means I'm in big trouble," the cabbie said.

"You think so?"

"I think so. Yeah."

"Doesn't matter," interrupted Dad. He handed me Helker's radio. "Some people found out first. We're being followed now."

I looked behind. There was another car at a polite distance behind. A blue Ford sedan. "That Ford?"

Dad shook his head. "No. Two cars back."

"How can you tell they're following?"

"They are."

"Should I be upset by all of this?" asked the cabbie.

"Yes," said Dad.

"What about me?" asked the woman.

"No."

"What's the problem?" asked the cabbie.

Dad asked, "How would you like to make a hundred-dollar tip?"

"I'd like to make it legally."

"All you have to do is observe the speed limit. Pay attention to all the pertinent traffic laws. And lose them."

"I'll give it a shot."

"That may prove to be a bad choice of words."

The cabbie winced.

Dad looked at me. He was shaking his head. "I'm sorry about all of this, Patty. I really am. I should have left you in Indiana. I shouldn't have dragged you into this."

I looked at Dad. That's who he was in that instant. And in that instant I was telling the truth when I said, "I'm not Patty."

"What?"

"She's still back there. With Doug."

Dad smiled, but it was weak. "Yeah. I guess that's so."

"Okay. So what's going to happen?"

Dad nodded, looking back. "Do you remember complaining to me about how complicated life is?"

"Yes." I used to complain about that all the time.

Dad nodded again. "You were always worried about school or some guy, about driving or the school play. . . ."

"Yes."

"Well, life is simpler than that now."

I looked back, trying to see the car that was following us.

Dad said, "Either they are going to catch us and take us to jail, or they are not."

They didn't catch us.

This upset Dad, but I didn't understand why. I don't claim to be brilliant, but it didn't take much in the way of brains to figure out that if we turned on Helker's radio we could listen in on the people following us, know just where they would be waiting and what spots to avoid. Still, Dad was unimpressed. The meter in the cab read $27.00 when Dad tossed a wad of bills over the seat. Next he apologized to the woman beside him. Then he said, "We're getting out at the next light. Cabbie, keep driving. You can brief the cops on your own time."

The cabbie was still digging through the bills as he drove. "There's almost three hundred bucks here. . . ."

"Yeah. Cover this lady's cab fare with that, too."

"No problem."

"I didn't figure there would be."

We were in downtown Bloomington, and the sun was fading fast. I was still amazingly calm inside. So calm, in fact, that I was just a little worried; maybe all of my emotions had short-circuited. What if it was impossible for me to ever again feel fear or nervousness? Would that be good or bad?

We stopped at the next red light and Dad kicked

open the door, pushing me out. "Leave the radio," he said. I did, wondering why — I still thought it could have come in handy for listening to the bad guys. Dad wanted nothing to do with it. We ran across the halted traffic, through the headlights, without bothering to close the taxi door behind us. There was a thick crowd of shoppers on the corner, in front of a department store.

This was obviously part of Dad's plan. We pushed our way into the crowd. A fat woman dragging three whining kids complained when Dad squeezed past her. I followed, muttering "Excuse me, excuse me, please." We cut through a side street and stepped quickly down the block to the next corner. We crissed and crossed for what seemed like a mile, winding up in front of a bakery across the street from a Woolworth's. Dad was looking around and behind us.

Down a ways, maybe four blocks or so, was a wide parking lot for several shops and a movie theater.

Dad nodded then. "Let's go to a movie."

"What?"

"A movie. Let's go to a movie."

So we did.

Why not?

I wanted to go to *A Case of Rivalry*, but it was half over, so we wound up getting tickets for *The Greenhouse Effect*, which had been on for only five minutes. It was a "Last Man on Earth" story, where everybody but the hero had been driven insane by the effects of germ warfare. There were plenty of action scenes, but I had suffered through enough action scenes of my own, and I didn't pay total attention to it. I almost fell asleep. Dad kept his eyes glued to the screen, but I knew from experience that when he paid that much attention to anything, he was actually ignoring it. He wasn't thinking about the movie at all.

I can't say I was surprised, but all the same it was beginning to worry me. Apparently my fear and worry system had not been short-circuited after all, merely numbed by battering after battering. I didn't know what upset me more: Dad being casual about crime or Dad being upset by it. Things had gone from one extreme to another, and they were crazy extremes to have to deal with.

When we finally left the theater around eight, it was cold outside. Dad zipped up his jacket and looked around the parking lot. People were already going in for the next show. Dad said finally, "This is too easy."

"What?"

"This is too easy. We're getting places too easily."

"Easy? Are you crazy? I almost had a heart attack today."

Dad shook his head. "Think about it. I just walk away from U.S. marshals at a truck stop. You ditch the FBI . . . twice. We just happen to get hold of their radio —"

"I blinded the guy."

"Yeah. Still."

"I really nailed him."

Dad frowned at me. "So what made you think to do it?"

I had been wondering about that myself. "I don't know. When I saw he couldn't get anyone on the radio, I just . . ."

"You just went for it?"

"I don't know. I guess I did."

"You think pretty fast."

"So do you, I guess."

Dad laughed. "Yeah. Right."

As we walked across the parking lot, Dad kept shaking his head. "Quick thinking or not, something is very wrong about all of this."

"Maybe we're just smart. Or lucky."

"I don't believe in luck, and if we're so smart, why are we running?"

"Because they won't let us stop?"

Dad looked at me, but he kept walking. I followed. A breeze shuddered through, and it felt even colder than before. "So where are we going?"

"Away from here. I don't know yet."

"Are we taking the train? Like you said?"

"No. It has to be a car again. They'll be watching the train station."

"Won't there be roadblocks?"

"You ever try to put a roadblock on an interstate? And make it work?"

"No."

"Few people have."

I was thinking weird thoughts. "Could it maybe be the CIA? Like all the people said?"

"What?"

I looked around to make sure that nobody was following or listening. "I read that big article. 'The Sandman and Killjoy.'"

"Wonderful. Did you see the movie?"

"*The what?*"

"The movie. It was great. I saw it three times. Starred James Franciscus and Bobby Darin."

"You're kidding."

"No. I'm not."

I thought about that a second. "A lot of people said the CIA broke you out of prison."

"A lot of people said a lot of things, Patty."

"It's Karen."

"What?"

"My name's Karen. Right?"

He looked over, smiled. "So it is. So what are you thinking, *Karen?*"

"Maybe the CIA is helping us."

"Not likely."

"But . . ."

"But what?"

"But Helker's FBI."

"Who?"

"The guy who grabbed me. He's FBI. A special agent, he said."

"And?"

"And before, the first time in South Bend, Helker said that U.S. marshals chase escaped convicts."

"Okay," said Dad. "So maybe the FBI thinks I'm kidnapping you. That's a federal offense."

I shook my head. "He thinks I was in on everything all along."

Dad shrugged. "I don't follow you. . . ."

"You said yourself everything's too easy. Maybe they're not trying very hard because the guys who know where we are aren't supposed to be here in the first place." I had to smile at that: I was proud of having figured one out myself.

Dad gave it some thought. "Yeah, but all it would take would be a telephone tip . . ." His voice trailed off, and we walked some more. Then he said, "So what else did the article say?"

"What?"

"What else did it say about my escape?"

"Nothing. Hardly anything."

"Did you know I hurt someone?"

I hesitated.

"Well, it's true."

I didn't say anything.

"There were three of us leaving together. Only it didn't work out that way. Vince never really wanted to go, I guess. Not really. He and Quinby got into a fight. It was crazy—right in the middle of everything, they're fighting. Quinby screaming he was yellow and . . . anyway, Quinby hurt Vince pretty

124

bad, broke his arm and face. I thought he was going to kill him, so I had to stop him somehow. I smashed him across the back with a heavy wrench. Hard."

"How hard?" I could barely speak.

"Harder than I had to, I guess. He didn't die, but he came close. I don't think he ever walked again."

I looked away.

"You have to understand that this was no nice guy off the street. He was a killer. A *murderer*. He probably would have killed Vince if I hadn't grabbed the wrench."

I swallowed. "But you were helping this murderer escape from prison with you?"

Dad took a breath, then nodded. "Yeah. I was. I didn't care. I'd do it today."

I shivered.

"I'm not going to lie to you again, Patty. Ever."

"Okay." We walked further, deeper into the dark. Away from the streetlights. "Why did the article say the CIA must have helped you escape?"

He thought about it. "Everybody was so absolutely convinced I couldn't have pulled it off on my own. Who knows? Maybe I couldn't."

"What do you mean?"

"Maybe they did help me. Maybe I just never knew about it."

"That's what I'm asking, then. Why would the CIA have helped you?"

Dad looked grim. "Why not? I helped them."

"What?"

"Alan and I were amateurs, baby. There was no way we should have gotten away with what we did for as long as we did. The CIA had to know. I think they used us."

"Used you for what?"

"*Disinformation.* They let us give the guy some information that wasn't true. False data. But in order to make this disinformation look real, they also had to let a lot of top-secret stuff go. Stuff they shouldn't have. Stuff the Soviets would know was far too valuable to be given to them *knowingly.* This kind of thing would make all the fake information look absolutely real."

"I thought you didn't know the man you gave the stuff to was a Russian."

Dad shrugged. "I guess maybe I knew. Deep down. Alan said some things that scared me. But like I said, it really didn't matter to me who he was giving the stuff to."

"So why would the CIA help you because of that?"

"Because not everything Alan and I did came up at my trial. A lot of stuff was left out. Stuff that would have made Congress crazy if I started to talk about it."

We stopped at a corner. The lights of Bloomington stretched out in front of us. A used car lot was across the street. GEORGE SAYLES — SALES IS MY LAST NAME!

Dad looked at me. "We need a car."

"Are you going to buy one?"

"It wouldn't do any good. We would still need plates for it."

"Can't you drive for so many days on the dealer's tags?"

"We'd need to show identification. Besides, I don't have that much money left."

"So what are you going to do?"

"Let's keep walking."

We started right, along a side street leading up a slight hill. I watched Dad. He seemed lost in his own mind, so I asked, "What are you thinking?"

"I'm wondering who it is that's helping us."

"So you think I'm right? You think somebody is helping us?"

"Yes, I think you're right. They want us to get away for now. Maybe they intend to get us later."

"Why?"

"It has to be the money."

"Money?"

"Yeah. You have to understand something about all of this weird CIA stuff, baby. The papers and drawings Alan and I were messing with are so old now that none of it matters. Do you know what the most sophisticated thing we gave up was?"

I shook my head. I never really had understood.

"Calculators. The technology to build pocket computers."

"You're kidding."

"I'm not. That was a big deal back in the sixties, before you could pick one up in every drugstore. Or get one free with a car wash."

I shivered, but it was probably from the cold. "So why do you think they let us go?"

"It has to be the money."

"You mean the money in the magazine article? The money the FBI wants so badly?"

Dad nodded. "All this money you thought I stole somewhere was mine. I kept about five thousand dollars in a secret hiding place for just such an emergency. I used to have two stashes of five thousand each. Until last year."

I gasped.

Dad laughed. "Yeah, that was my money."

The year before, three teenagers playing around a wooden bridge across a creek outside Michigan City had found a metal box containing five thousand dollars in old bills. It made the newspapers and the radio stations. Nobody claimed the money, and the boys ended up receiving $1,666.66 each. Before taxes.

"Wow," I said. "But if they want the money, why haven't they just robbed us?"

Dad was still smiling, but he shook his head. He seemed to be scanning the dark street ahead of us. "They don't want the money that I have on me. That's chicken feed. There's less than a thousand of it left, anyway. But they know that somewhere I have another ninety thousand."

"You really do have all that money?"

"Safely hidden."

"And that's why you think they're leaving us alone?"

Dad nodded. "Some less than reputable law enforcement official has decided to let us slip through the net. That would take too much coordination, too much confusion, to be anybody local. It has to be someone federal. Either a U.S. marshal or somebody with the FBI . . . or CIA."

"So they don't really want us anymore?"

"Oh, a lot of people probably still do. If we get caught by some local cop or dedicated marshal this other guy's plan is messed up, and I go to jail anyway. But this guy must figure I'm smart enough to avoid small-time cops and feds. He just wants me to get desperate and go straight to the money."

"Will you?"

"Of course. What else can I do?"

"But what happens when you go to it?"

Dad shrugged.

"Will they kill you?"

"Not without a fight."

"Where did you get the gun?"

Dad smiled again. "Do you remember Mr. Lowell?"

"Back in Michigan City?"

"Yes."

I nodded. Mr. Lowell had been our next-door neighbor for years before we moved to our new house on Henry Street.

"I broke into his house. It was the first place I went

after I got the car. I took the gun out of his desk drawer."

"Is it loaded?"

"Absolutely."

I didn't respond. Dad had stopped walking — we were standing near a red Firebird. It was a beautiful new car, sitting ignored out in front of an auto parts store. Dad was looking up and down the street. "We have a long way to go."

All I said was "I'm cold."

"I know." Dad nodded toward the car. "So am I."

NINE

Fifteen days later we were in San Bavispe, California. We had been there three days. About seven hundred and twenty miles east of San Diego, San Bavispe was located about a hundred miles east of the coast and fifty miles north of the Mexican border, just south of a hilly range called Chocolate Mountains. Seriously, they were really called that. The roadside motel where we were staying was called Cactus Place. The motel was horseshoe-shaped around a blacktopped parking lot and had ice and soda machines humming loudly outside room 21.

We were in room 19.

The trip had been weird. Dad would drive nonstop for sixteen, eighteen hours and then rest for two days in some odd place. Driving, he didn't say much; he became this distant, obsessed figure. But when we stopped, he was Dad again. I couldn't get used to the changes. Once I forgot to adjust, and as we drove I was asking him endless questions. Suddenly he just turned and barked, "*Shut up, please.*" I jumped when he yelled, and he said he was sorry, but I didn't forget again.

I guess he was doing a lot of thinking.

We spent our first morning at Six Flags Over Mid-America, the big amusement park. This was Dad's present to me for dyeing my hair black. I wore my make-up just about all the time now. Dad said I was growing up hard.

After Six Flags, we drove like crazy in a newly acquired car until we came to Augusta, Kansas, which is just outside of Wichita. We bounced all over the map with no real destination, it seemed. Between Bloomington, Illinois, and San Bavispe, California, we passed through seven states, and except for the amusement park in Missouri and Hoover Dam in Nevada, we hardly saw anything but diners, gas stations, and motel rooms. We spent one night in Las Vegas, but it was Las Vegas, New Mexico, not Nevada, and there is definitely a difference. I guess I was having a good time with my wild geography lesson. I saw Enid, Oklahoma, and Amarillo, Texas. Albuquerque, New Mexico, and Flagstaff, Arizona. It was exciting: Take the feeling of ringing a strange doorbell and running off, and multiply that feeling about a thousand times. It was life on the edge.

I became more used to Dad, but still it's a weird feeling to keep watch while your father steals a car. Between Bloomington and San Bavispe, we went through seven cars. Dad said it was necessary. The first was the red Firebird, a car I loved. I was sorry when we dumped it. The last was a Volkswagen Rabbit with Arizona plates. Dad got rid of it on our first day in San Bavispe, but I kept the Billy Joel tapes we found in it. I still don't know why.

The second day in San Bavispe, Dad gave me twenty dollars and permission to go looking around town if I wanted. He held the bill back for just a second when I reached for it. "Just try to keep sort of a low profile."

"I will." And I did. I also managed to explore almost the entire downtown in just a few hours. It wasn't exactly Michigan City or the Merrillville Mall, but then again it wasn't Augusta, Kansas, either. I walked up and down streets looking into store windows. I got it into my head that I wasn't just shopping but scouting around. Spying on the place, seeing what I could see. The town had a Mexican atmosphere about it. Mexican food was everywhere. San Bavispe was about half the size of Michigan City, I guessed, but it was large enough to disappear in if you wanted to. I figured that was what Dad wanted to do. Disappear.

Myself, I couldn't see spending the rest of my days living there under an assumed name. Forever wasn't even a question. Not then. I was looking forward to the time when the running would end and everything would be sorted out. Maybe it was just a fantasy, but I wanted to be Patty Meely again.

Another problem was developing, and I couldn't think of a way around it. Now that we had stopped, apparently for a while, I wanted my dad back, but instead he stayed inside himself, the guy who had driven us here. He seemed involved in something and almost unfriendly. I figured it was nerves. It would pass when his mind settled.

What was I thinking? I wondered. I was wandering around in a small town in California, hoping my car-thief/escaped-convict father would calm down and tell me what we were going to do next. It was insane.

After a few hours I walked back to the Cactus Place. The motel was about two miles from the center of town. I was watching television when Dad got back from wherever he had been. He seemed surprised that I hadn't bought anything.

"Nothing to buy," I said.

"You could have got me a newspaper."

"I didn't know you wanted one."

"Next time try to think ahead a little. Okay?" He sounded almost snotty.

I shrugged. "Sorry."

He sat down at the desk and started to flip through the telephone directory.

I looked at him. "So what are we going to do now?"

"What?"

"Where are we going?"

"Nowhere yet."

"I just wondered."

"Don't you trust me?"

"What?"

Dad looked me hard in the eye. "Don't you trust me?"

"Yeah. I guess."

"You *guess?*" He hissed the word.

"What's wrong?"

"Nothing." He slammed the phone book shut. "Not a thing."

I looked at the television screen. I could hear Dad moving around behind me. I looked up toward the mirror on the far side of the room. In it I could see him taking off his shoes. He had bleached the roots of his hair again, and the stubble on his face was growing into a beard. A few more days in the sun and he would look like a beach bum. The girl with the jet-black hair and her beach-bum father. Only there was no beach in San Bavispe. I figured that since we weren't running, the pressure of it all was on his shoulders. I sighed. "How long can we keep this up?"

Dad dropped his sock on the floor. He was barefoot. "You're going to drive yourself crazy thinking about this."

I shrugged. "I'm already crazy."

"No, you're not."

I turned back to the television and turned the sound up very, very loud. Fine. If he didn't want to talk about any of it, neither did I. The room reverberated with bells and hysterical excitement as the lady on the screen won a new automobile on a game show. It was amazing. No matter how far you ran, the game shows were always one step ahead of you. The picture and the sound blipped out suddenly. The room was silent. I turned around and stood up.

Dad had killed everything with the remote control box. He set the box quietly down on the nightstand by his bed. It was his turn to sigh. "I'm sorry."

"So am I."

"I just can't stop."

"I know. But you should. You have to."

"Patty —"

"What happened to Karen? Isn't that who you made me into? Are you ashamed of it now?"

"What do you think will happen now, Patty? Do you think they're going to just let us start living again?"

I didn't know what to say. I felt something weird, pulling and pushing inside. I felt stupid and superior at the same time. I didn't know the answer to his question, or maybe I did but just couldn't admit it.

Dad drove the last nail in. "I don't remember all of these complaints when you were chasing around that Bloomington mall with money in both fists."

I shivered, turned away. I was ready to lose it.

"What should I do, Patty? Spend the rest of my life rotting in jail? Never see you again?"

I cringed at the thought. "No."

"I know this is all bad for the brain, honey, but I'll get us out of it. Right now we just have to keep surviving."

"But how? What's next? You said yourself the money was running low. Are you going to start robbing banks?"

"Money is not going to be a problem. I promise. But remember something — once outside the law, always outside it."

"Is that the way you've always thought?"

Dad grimaced. "I tried to be perfect once. For you. It doesn't work. This is what happens because of it. You can't try to live your life by two sets of rules."

"Daddy . . ." I couldn't believe it; my head was spinning again. "I'm scared. This is all wrong. Was everything you taught me growing up just a lie?"

"No!" His voice was harsh. "It was real and important for the world we used to live in. But they kicked us both out of that world. So those rules no longer apply to us."

"Wrong is wrong. Isn't it?"

"Those are easy words. Easy words."

I tried again to understand. To really understand. I sat down and said, "So what are we doing here?"

"Waiting."

The answer dawned on me. "The money is here. Isn't it?"

Dad didn't hesitate. "Yes. Somewhere between here and San Diego."

"But how could you have . . ."

"I used to live in California."

"Oh."

"The only problem is I can't go for the money until I'm sure I'm being watched."

"Until you're sure you *are* being watched?"

Dad nodded.

"That's crazy," I said. "I thought you didn't want them to know where the money was."

"I don't. But it's impossible to really know when you're *not* being watched. So instead you wait until you know exactly who is following, who is watching. Then you lose them."

I couldn't help smiling. This man Casper Pelling may not have been the Doug Meely who worked at the steel mill and bowled on his days off, but he was a very clever guy. I couldn't help feeling proud of him. "So where are we going when you get the money?"

"I've been thinking about South America."

"What?"

"Would you like to live in Buenos Aires? For a while?"

"We don't speak Spanish."

"Fine. We'll have fun learning."

"It would be hard."

"Nothing worthwhile comes easy."

I frowned.

Dad laughed. A more happy laugh than he had in days. "Okay. What about Australia?"

"Australia?"

"Kangarooland. Yes. Or New Zealand."

I guess I smirked.

"Don't you want to go? You said yourself that you wanted to get away from this place."

"Could we go just like that?"

"Well, no. We'd need passports. That would take a few days at least. I'd have to get money to pay for them."

"Are you ready to go for the money yet?"

"Not yet. Soon."

That was Dad's plan, and I couldn't decide how I felt about it.

The next day I walked into town again, looking around at things I had already seen. I resolved not to go back to the Cactus Place until I had spent at least part of the money Dad had given me.

There was sort of an outdoor market in the downtown area. The weather was cool but not cold; the sky was sharp blue and clear. I was standing by a rack of summer dresses, reduced in price, which had been set up in front of a clothing store. I only half heard the approaching engine and didn't think anything of it until a woman screamed; that's when I swung around.

A motorcycle, riding fast on the sidewalk, buzzed by me, inches from running me down. I felt the suction pulling me as it passed.

"Hey! Hey, stop him!" The storekeeper was on the street, shaking a fist and shouting after the biker as he disappeared down the street. It was only then dawning on me how close I had come to being splattered. The woman who had screamed was standing next to me. She was about thirty and wore tan slacks and shirt. Her hair was as black as mine and her eyes were hard. "He almost killed you," she said.

"Almost."

"I hope the cops get him."

I didn't say anything.

About an hour later and a mile and a half away, the motorcycle buzzed me again. I got a much better look this time. I was sitting on a bench in front of a Dairy Queen, eating a chili dog and sipping a soda. I wasn't really hungry, but I felt I had to spend some of the money. For Dad, just to keep things calm. A sleek blue motorcycle streaked by quickly. I almost missed it that time, too, since it was on the street, but I saw it make a U-turn. It roared back toward me, as if my assassination had been the idea all along.

I saw it charging at me, and for a split second I was terrified.

Here we go again.

The bike throttled back, though, and stopped by the curb in front of me. The rider was wearing a black leather jacket, jeans, and a dark visored helmet. He raised the visor and switched off his engine. It sputtered into silence.

He was about seventeen, with dark eyebrows, clear blue eyes, and a shy smile. "Hello." He spoke quietly.

I blinked at him.

He looked around and seemed to shrug the world

away. He couldn't seem to help smiling, and scratched at his chin, which had just the faintest stubble of beard. "I just wanted to say I'm sorry."

I frowned and set aside my chili dog.

"So I'm sorry. About all that." He grimaced for just a second.

I nodded. "Do you always run people over with your motorcycle?"

"No. I nearly always miss."

"Nearly always?"

He pulled off a glove and offered me his right hand. "My name is David. David Borrego."

I didn't shake. "So?"

He frowned, sat back on his bike. "How old are you?"

"How old are you?"

"I asked first."

"And I didn't answer because it's none of your business."

"Okay," he said. "I'll be eighteen in January."

"Am I supposed to be impressed?"

"You asked."

"So I did."

"How come I never see you in school?" He was smiling again.

"How do you know I go to the same school as you?"

"There's only one high school in town."

"I could be here just for the day."

"Are you?"

"No."

"So why aren't you at school? Are you sick?"

"Is that an accusation?"

He laughed. "No. But everybody has to go to school."

"I have a tutor."

He looked impressed. "Really? Are you rich?"

"No."

"Then why do you have a tutor?"

"He's my father."

"Oh."

I looked at his motorcycle. I asked, "Are you a criminal?"

He looked shocked. "What?"

"Where I come from only criminals ride their motorcycles on sidewalks."

"I had to. I got run off the road by that van."

"What van?"

"The one nobody else saw. Everyone was too busy watching me ride on the sidewalk."

I looked at him doubtfully.

"Really. It was either hit the van, wipe out and crash, or ride on the sidewalk for a minute."

"You might have killed somebody."

He shook his head. "So where are you from?"

"New Zealand."

"I don't believe you're from New Zealand."

"Why not?"

"You don't have an accent."

"I speak with an Earth accent. I'd sound really funny if you were a Martian."

He nodded at that. Then he asked, "Do you like motorcycles?"

"I think they're dangerous."

"So do I."

"So why do you ride one?"

"Because I'm very careful and because I know how. Do you want to learn?"

"Absolutely not."

"Would you like to see me jump something?"

"Absolutely not. What do you jump?"

"Mostly garbage cans and stuff. A week from Saturday I'm going to jump five cars in the road and track show."

"In the what?"

"The road and track show at the fairgrounds. Aren't you going?"

"I don't know anything about it."

"You have to go."

"I don't *have* to do anything."

"Everybody in town will be there. You can watch me ride."

"Why would I want to watch you ride?"

He shrugged. "I thought you might. What's your name?"

"Cassandra Dervish."

"Is that a New Zealand name?"

"Yes."

"What part of New Zealand are you from?"

"The south part."

"Name one city in New Zealand."

143

"There are so many I don't know where to begin."

He nodded slowly then. "Do you ever tell the truth, Cassandra Dervish?"

"Do you ever get off that motorcycle?"

"I'm late."

"For what?"

"Ah! You do care!"

"I could care less."

"You mean you could *not* care less."

"No. I care a little. I could care more, but I could also care less."

"You're funny."

"Thank you. You look pretty weird yourself."

He nodded again. His smile showed a capped tooth. "Can I call you?"

"Can you call me what?"

"On the phone."

"I don't have a phone."

"Don't you trust me?"

"I don't even know you."

He sighed. "Okay. Will you tell me where you live?"

"New Zealand. I already said."

"I meant in town. Where are you staying?"

"Here and there."

"I've been there. Nice place."

"I think so."

"Would you like a ride over?"

"No thanks."

He seemed to hesitate just a second, but then he hopped up and down and started his motorcycle. He shouted over the engine, "Will I see you around town?"

I shrugged. "Will you be looking?"

"Definitely."

"Then I guess you might."

He nodded, pulling his visor down. "I'll talk to you later, Cassandra Dervish."

TEN

A few days later, on a Monday afternoon, Dad slipped back into the motel room to take a shower.

He had warned me the evening before that he would not be back until well into the next day. I was, of course, terrified. I spent the evening and the next morning hanging around the room reading a paperback I bought in a little store by the motel office. I ate lunch in the room: two sandwiches from the lunch wagon in the motel lot. When Dad returned he didn't say anything, and I was afraid to ask. After about twenty minutes he came out of the bathroom in his new blue slacks, drying his hair with a towel. The dark roots were starting to grow back in, but his bleached beard was coming along fine.

"I'm afraid we're going to have to postpone our trip for a while," he said.

It had never seemed to me like a definite plan anyway, but I asked, "Why?"

146

"Some things have come up."

I felt even more frightened. "What happened?"

"Nothing — just some details I want to see settled before leaving the country."

"You have me worried now."

"Don't be. Just trust me. Okay?"

"Okay."

He flipped the towel away. Reaching for a clean shirt, he asked, "Did you watch television today?"

"What's to watch?"

"I thought there might have been some news I missed."

I shrugged. "Do you want me to turn it on?"

"No. Not if it bothers you."

"Why would it bother me?"

He didn't answer. After he finished buttoning his shirt, he started slowly. "Patty . . ."

"Promise me something."

He looked at me, surprised. I was surprised, too. It had just blurted out — I hadn't even really known what I was going to say. He asked, "What?"

"Promise me that if they catch me, you'll go."

His eyes narrowed. "What?"

"You know they're following us. . . ."

"I don't know that yet."

"Yes you do. You just don't talk about it."

After a minute he relented. "Okay . . ."

I stood up and walked around the room. "I'm not as good at all this as you are. I just want you to promise that if they catch me you won't hang around, trying to think of a way to get me out. Because if you do you'll get caught, too."

"Patty . . ."

"Let's be for real, okay?"

He thought about it. "Okay."

"What will they do to me if I get picked up?"

"Nothing, I —"

"No." I raised a hand. "At the very least I'll be on probation in some foster home. I'm an accomplice to all of this, right? I might even wind up in a reform school. Or juvenile jail."

He said nothing.

"But," I said, emphasizing the *but*, "whatever they do to me will be temporary. A couple years at most. Two. Maybe three. Right?"

At first nothing. Then he looked away.

"But if they catch you, it's fifty years. Or more. Am I right?"

"Right."

"Not to mention the stuff you don't talk about. The people you think will kill you."

"Yes."

"So promise if they catch me you'll leave."

"I can't leave you."

"Promise me."

He was silent another moment. Finally he said, "Okay. But only if you'll promise me something first."

"What?"

"I'm going to hide some money away for you —"

148

"No."

"Listen. It'll only be part of it. I'll tell you where it is. It'll be someplace you can't miss, if you know what you're looking for."

"No."

"Patty, if there are problems, you'll need money. You'll need money to survive."

"No!" I tried to make it sound final.

"Do I have to go over everything again? Okay. Here's what you have out there. Aside from the Renegades, the bogus FBI or CIA types out after the cash, you've got every law enforcement agency in America after us. After you and me. Patty, you can't ever go home again."

I blinked.

Dad said softly, "I thought you realized that."

I swallowed. "Eventually —"

He didn't let me finish. "Patty, if you ever show your face in Michigan City again, you're going to jail. Every day you get deeper in this, and every day you get older. The older you are, the less sympathetic they'll be when they catch up to you. If you got arrested now, you might do three years in reform school. If they nail you when you're twenty, you might get stuck in prison for five years. Or more."

"What's going to happen?"

"I don't know. I'm working on this all the time, getting closer to something. You have to believe me. But we need to be prepared for the worst."

I didn't say anything. I just stared at his face as he explained it all. I listened as he said my life was absolutely, entirely over.

He took another breath. "I'm sorry I got you into all of this. It was a mistake, I know that now. Maybe I was fooling myself all along, thinking somebody in my position could raise a daughter."

I shook my head. "Daddy . . ."

He asked me to listen. "After your mother died, I thought —"

"Daddy, please."

"She never knew. Did I say that? Your mother never knew about Casper Pelling and his problems."

Tears were starting to form in Dad's eyes, and his words were choking over. He had seemed so strong through all of this that I had assumed his feelings were cool. Or worse. I had assumed that he had no feelings.

He said, "You know if we split up, we'll never get to see each other again."

"I know."

"Just no way. How could we find each other? We've already used our secret hiding place."

"I know."

"I never wanted it to be this way."

"I know."

"I . . . I never wanted to be a bad person, Patty. But you can never go back."

I nodded finally. "I know that now."

"I'm so sorry. I'm sorry that you had to learn that. Nobody should have to learn that."

"It's all right."

He started to pull himself together. Stood straight. "So remember. There will be money. I'll tell you where later. If anything comes up, anything at all, you take the cash and go. Get as far away as fast as possible."

"But where can I go?"

"Anywhere you want, if you're smart. And you're smart. We both know that now."

I looked away.

"I don't even want to know where you might go," he said. "Just in case they drug me."

"Who are 'they'?"

"Any of them."

"Why can't we just give them the money? Get away from all of this?" I turned on him.

Dad's face was tight. "No. Absolutely not." He relaxed some. "It's been too far and too long. Besides, who would we give it to? What if more than one person wants it? Do I ask them to kill each other and use it as a prize?"

I grimaced.

Dad shrugged. "That's the way it is. Now I want your promise on this. I'll sleep better."

"Okay," I said. "I promise. But I really don't know what I'll do if it happens."

"You will survive. I know you'll do that much."

I wasn't pressing, but I had to ask the next question. "About how much longer will we be in town?"

Dad thought about it. "Maybe a week."

"No longer than that?"

"I don't think so. Why?"

"I was just wondering if we were going to be around on Saturday."

He thought about it. "I suppose we might be. Any particular reason?"

"Not really. If we're here I might want to go to the road and track show."

"The what?"

"It's out at the fairgrounds. Auto show, demolition derby, motorcycle stunts."

Dad raised an eyebrow. "Since when are you interested in auto shows?"

"I like the stunts."

He frowned.

"No big deal," I said. "If we're still here, I'll go. If not, no problem. Right?"

Dad slowly accepted this. "Right."

I turned back to my book.

"Patty?"

"Yes?"

He looked at me just a minute, then shook his head. "Never mind."

Later that afternoon he left the room, and so did I. I headed downtown. I told myself it was just for a walk, for some air, but I guess I was secretly hoping to run into the crazed motorcyclist again. David Borrego. But as I was walking through the center square, I started to get a nervous, queasy feeling in the pit of my stomach. I looked around me and thought I saw a head duck into a doorway.

Imagination?

I bought a small bag of apples from a fruit shop and kept walking. There weren't many people out and about, but I couldn't help feeling that I was being watched. Being followed. The figures were always in the corner of my eye, but whenever I turned . . . they were gone.

"You look spooked."

I jumped. I was walking past the Dairy Queen, where I had last seen him, and David Borrego was there. He was wiping the seat of his bike with a rag. "Easy, I don't bite hard."

I recovered and smiled. "I'm fine."

"You like apples." He gestured.

"Better than candy bars."

He nodded. "I was afraid you had gone back to New Zealand."

"We did. For dinner yesterday. We're back now."

"I'm glad."

"Are you?"

He lifted his helmet from the back of the bike. "Yeah, I am."

"Why?"

"Do I need a reason?"

"You might."

He just smiled and shook his head.

I looked around. "Are you late again today?"

"Sort of."

"So why aren't you hurrying to get where you're going?"

"I looked all weekend. I might not find you again."

"You might. Consider it a challenge."

"Why can't you just go out with me?"

"That would be too much of a challenge for you."

"Challenge me."

"Nope. It would be much too challenging."

"Please!"

I laughed. He looked so pathetic.

"What's so funny?"

I shook my head. "You."

"Thanks a lot."

"My dad doesn't let me go out on dates." I suspected that was probably true. Or certainly advisable, seeing how I was at the very least a federal criminal, wanted in fifty states. It occurred to me then what real complications might lie ahead for me. Obviously I was not getting married anytime soon. . . .

"Do you ever sneak out?" asked David Borrego.

I smirked. "Are you serious?"

"All I want to do is take you to a movie or something."

"Or something?"

He frowned.

"So why ask me?"

"Because you're the weirdest girl I ever met in my life."

"That's a wonderful reason."

"I think so."

"Okay. You want weird? Let's go on a date right now."

"Right now? I'm late for practice . . ."

"What kind of practice?"

"For my jump Saturday."

"Your decision."

"Hey!"

I started walking.

He called, "What about tomorrow?"

I looked back. "What about it?"

"Can we do it tomorrow? Tomorrow night?"

"Tomorrow afternoon."

"Okay. I'll skip practice."

"Is that safe?"

"Sure. I just have to let the guys know ahead of time."

I hesitated, then nodded. "Okay. Meet me here tomorrow. Dairy Queen. Three o'clock."

"Can't I pick you up?"

I shook my head.

He shrugged. "Okay. Where are we going?"

"To get me a driver's license."

"To what?"

"I need to get a driver's license. You can take me to wherever I need to go."

"We're going on a driver's license date?"

"You wanted weird. Stand up and accept."

He laughed. "Okay."

I smiled, myself. "You might just make it, kid."

"Thanks."

As I started to walk away, he called out again. "Hey!"

I called back. "Hey what?"

"What's your real name, anyway?"

I started to answer, then caught myself. Almost a biggie. Just a second. "Karen."

"Karen?"

"Karen Peterson."

He looked doubtful, climbing onto his bike. "You don't look like a Karen."

"I have a birth certificate to prove it."

"I believe you."

"Tomorrow I'll even have a driver's license."

"I believe you, I believe you." He put on his helmet and started his bike. "I really am late."

I turned away again. "Bye!"

"Hey!"

"This is getting old, kid!"

"You're beautiful, Karen Peterson!"

Inside I shivered. Karen Peterson. Would he have said that to Patricia Meely? Or Patricia Pelling? Patricia Pelling with the long, dirty brown hair and the criminal record? I said nothing else and kept walking, listening as the bike roared off. Then I turned and watched him disappear.

So I was alone again.

It was almost five, and I was still in town. Dad was probably back in the room, concerned. I needed to get back. A bus ran from town, and I decided to try to grab it. That was when I saw the man.

He looked *evil*.

He was on the other side of the street, directly across from me. He had long, stringy black hair, and he was looking me straight in the eye. I felt cold, out in the open. Vulnerable. He was wearing a gray sport coat with no tie, and he definitely looked out of place. As I watched him watching me, he calmly lit a cigarette and flicked the match away. Exhaled. He smiled at me.

I ran.

It was ending; it was ending. That was all I thought. I didn't know where I was going, but I was running. Taking harsh breaths. I stopped, ducked around a corner, and sneaked a look behind.

Nobody seemed to be following. There was no sign of Longhair.

I closed my eyes for a second. I had learned enough to realize that didn't mean a thing. Who was he? Who did he work for? Helker? The . . . what did Dad call them? The Renegades?

I looked around again, quickly. I felt like I was pushing at the edges of a small box that kept getting smaller. So this was paranoia.

It wasn't much fun.

My back was flat against the wall of a building. People were passing around me, and nobody seemed to take any notice. I remembered now the talk on

Helker's radio. If Helker was Viper, then maybe Longhair was Cobra. The insanity of it all was enough to drive you — well — crazy.

Edging along the building, I came to a set of lobby doors. It seemed a good idea to get off the street, so I pushed in. The building turned out to be the San Bavispe post office. Wonderful.

The air conditioning was cranked up, and it was quite cool. I took several quick breaths, trying to calm myself. Was I so paranoid that I was imagining things? I had my new look. Maybe Longhair was just some guy who thought I was cute or sexy. I frowned. Don't flatter yourself.

The smell of paper and glue ticked my nostrils, and I looked around. It wasn't a big post office; all business transacted in the one lobby. I stayed close to the doors, keeping watch. A woman was at the one open window, mailing some packages. I looked around some more. I caught a glimpse of the bulletin board and froze.

WANTED BY THE FBI
AND THE UNITED STATES MARSHALS SERVICE

It was my picture.

ELEVEN

Of course it wasn't *really* my picture.

Not anymore.

They had taken my eighth-grade class photo and reproduced it in stark black and white. It looked pretty peculiar, me with the long hair I had then, smiling my schoolgirl smile above the instructions of who to contact with any information as to my whereabouts. Next to my picture was a pair of mug shots of the Sandman. They weren't pictures of Dad; they were the images of some sinister creep misusing his face. One was a full-front shot and the other a right profile. In the full-front, he was holding an identification card: HZ 113478. I stared at his tired face, into the eyes. They were unreadable.

I left the post office in a hurry.

Dad met me in the doorway of the motel room, but I pushed him back inside, telling him about the poster and Longhair.

The poster didn't surprise him, but he was very

curious about the man. "Are you sure he was following you?"

I shook my head. "No. But he was looking at me like I was his long-lost love."

Dad frowned. "It might be nothing."

"You don't believe that."

"No."

There was soda in our tiny refrigerator, and I opened one for myself. I couldn't believe how thirsty I was; I downed half the can before speaking. "What are we going to do?"

Dad shrugged. He was thinking. "I don't know. Maybe we should leave."

"No —" I caught myself saying it.

Dad blinked, looking at me. "What?"

I didn't know how to explain it. "Do we have to run?"

"What else can we do?"

"We can give them the money."

"*What?*"

"*Yes.* If that's all they want, then let's give it to them. Maybe they'll leave us alone."

"We already talked about that."

"Dad, we're *always* talking about this. Let's just end it!"

"We will. But not like this."

I finished the soda, thinking. "Well, it can't be the cops. Longhair can't be legit."

"Why not?"

"Because real cops would have grabbed us by now. Right?"

Dad shrugged again. "Maybe. I guess."

"So all we have to do for now is be careful. Right?"

"Patty, they've got everything on their side."

"Not everything."

Dad looked at me again.

"The money," I said. "Isn't that what this is all about now?"

"It's always about money."

"Right. And you know where it is, and they don't. All you have to do is wait."

"Yes. But wait for what?"

"Wait for us to think of something."

"I don't think it'll be that simple," he said. "The best bet might be to move on. Come back later. A year from now. Maybe more."

"No." I said it again.

"And why not?"

"I'm sick of running."

Dad sighed. "So am I. We'll see."

I nodded again. It was true that I was sick of running; it was true that I was scared of who Longhair might turn out to be. But I was also afraid that if we left now, I might never see David Borrego again. And I was surprised how much that bothered me.

We didn't talk about much of anything until later that night, when Dad came out of the bathroom drying his newly bleached hair. He set the gun in the middle of his bed. "Come here," he said. "I'm going to show you how this works."

"*What?*"

"I'm going out this evening. You're right. We're not going to run anymore. But that involves more risks."

"No, wait, Daddy. I just meant . . ."

"I know." He tossed the towel aside. "Everything will be all right. Just listen. Just in case." He sat down on the bed and patted it for me to sit as well. I did. He lifted the pistol and pressed a catch. Then he pulled the clip out, which contained the bullets. "Watch." He snapped something back and showed it to me.

"This is the chamber," he said. "It's empty now. There's no clip in the weapon and no round in the chamber, which means this gun is safe." He aimed the gun across the room and snapped the trigger. I jumped. Nothing happened. He smiled.

"In order to make this gun fire, you have to do two things. First, load it." He held the clip up for me. "This holds eight bullets. It snaps in like this." He slammed the clip into the gun's butt. "See? It locks into place."

I nodded.

"This gun is loaded, but it still won't fire. That's because it's an automatic. You have to chamber the first round by hand. Like this." He pulled the front of the gun forward and let it snap back. "I just snapped the bolt, chambering a round. This gun can kill now."

Kill. The word just hung there.

"Here's how you make the gun safe again," he said. He reversed the whole process, and handed me the empty pistol. "All told, it should take about five seconds to go from cold to deadly."

I swallowed. "Please. Why are you doing this?"

Dad held the gun out. "Try it."

I hesitated. Slowly, fumbling, I took it.

"Don't be afraid," he said. "If you have respect for a weapon, you'll never have any problems."

I held it steady. It was heavy. "Like this?" I asked.

Dad nodded. I went through the motions, not even thinking about them. Dad corrected my mistakes along the way. Finally I was sitting there, beside him on the bed, with a solid bit of steel capable of killing a man three times in three seconds.

Dad took the gun back and made it safe again. "I'm leaving it here with you tonight."

I felt like I was in a daze. Covered with gauze, wrapped in cotton. Everything around me seemed fuzzy. "Why?"

Dad placed the gun carefully in the nightstand drawer, and beside it, the clip. "It's like you said. We're finished running."

"But what's going to happen?"

"Nothing."

"I know you don't believe that."

"*Stop telling me what I think!*"

I jumped.

Dad grabbed my shoulders. "I'm sorry. Really.

163

Nothing is going to happen. But I can't leave here tonight with you sitting alone. Now you're not alone."

"Where are you going?"

He ignored me again. "If you hear anything outside, load the gun first. Then ask questions. If it's the police, drop the gun immediately. Don't even think about it."

"What if it's somebody else?"

Dad stared. "Don't even think about it."

I hesitated again. "This isn't the way it's supposed to be."

"I know. But this is the way it is. I'll be back as soon as I can. I promise."

And he left.

I just sat there, numbed. Numbed is an easy word; I had been numbed when the graysuits pounced on Dad. I felt like I was standing outside myself, watching, but powerless to even speak. And I was terrified at the same time. First Longhair, watching so calmly. Like he was confident, like he knew something I didn't. And now Dad and this craziness. What was going on here? First he tells me there's probably nothing to worry about, and next he's leaving me with a gun — just in case.

I stared at the drawer, then got up and paced the room. What was this turning into? *Bonnie and Clyde?* I saw that movie: Bonnie and Clyde both wound up dead. Was this heading in the same direction?

It wasn't cold, but I shivered. I got the next to last soda, and turned on the television. Watching the

164

sitcoms didn't help; the only image in my mind was of Dad and me lying in some ditch, dead.

The closed door looked very still.

Maybe it was time I left. Went on my own. I didn't need this; I didn't need to be around it. If it was selfish, so what? Maybe it was time to be selfish. I didn't want to die.

I thought about David Borrego and his motorcycle. Maybe he could help. He was taking me to get a driver's license the next day. Maybe he would just take me away.

Yeah. Maybe. I decided to sleep on it and make my decision in the morning. After I got the driver's license I would ask David about it. He was in for a shock. But could I trust him?

I kept looking at the drawer.

I was terrified, but at the same time fascinated. Drawn to it. I had never held a gun before, and it took some courage to open the drawer and pick it up again. Slick steel. Popping open the bolt, I double-checked the chamber to assure myself it was empty. I left the clip in the drawer. Walking around the room, I felt myself growing taller.

Yeah. Why not?

What was happening to me?

I drew a bead on the television newsman.

He was reading, calmly, ignorant of his danger: "A development in the Southwest Airlines flight attendants' strike is expected any hour now —"

Blam!

Goodbye, newsman.

Sick.

I looked at the gun, trailed my fingertips across it. What did this represent to Dad? Another threshold to cross? Would he wind up a murderer? I shuddered yet again. Would *I*?

I let my eyes go cold, and sighted across the chair. At the door. Whatever happens, happens. "Go ahead, kid," I said to the invisible intruder standing there. "Let me make my life more interesting. . . ."

The latch popped and the door opened. On reflex I squeezed the trigger. Had the gun been loaded, I would have killed him.

Dad stood there. He didn't say a word.

The gun fell to the carpet. Dad closed the door and walked over to pick it up. He stuck it in the drawer with the clip and then went into the bathroom. The only thing he said was "It's late."

I went to bed. Crying.

The next morning I woke up early. Dad sounded like he was in a good mood. The clock read 8:11 A.M., and I remembered that today was David Borrego day. I thought about my big decision but put it off. Dad was sorting through a stack of newspapers. An open package of doughnuts lay on the dresser top, next to a container of orange juice. Dad chirped a good morning my way.

After what had happened with the gun, I didn't know what to say. I had felt so tall with it. Now I felt about two inches high. Is that what guns did for you?

"It's really sunny outside today," Dad was saying. "Get up. Grab some orange juice. Better have a doughnut before I finish them all."

My mouth was dry, but I swallowed. "Why are you so happy?"

"Because things are progressing."

"What does that mean?"

He shrugged. "It means things are moving along."

"Are they?"

"They are indeed."

I looked away. "I . . . I'm sorry about last night."

Dad ignored that. He said, "I'm quite sure the two clowns following me last night were annoyed."

"What?"

He didn't answer the question. Not directly, anyway, which was getting more and more to be the case. "They're outside now," he said. "At least somebody is. And they definitely don't want to arrest me. Not yet, anyway."

"What does that mean?"

"I don't know." He looked at me brightly, tossing the papers aside. "You know what?"

I frowned. "What?"

"They'll probably make *another* movie about me. Imagine that!" He laughed.

"What are they thinking about?" I looked toward the window. The shades were drawn, despite Dad's announcement of what a sunny morning it was.

He was still laughing. "I really don't know. Last night I did everything but flag them down and turn myself in. No response."

"What?"

He smiled. "It's okay. At the end of round three, just score it Casper three, world nothing."

My blood went cold. *Casper.* Not Doug Meely or this new person he was supposed to be, Lou Peterson. He thought of himself as Casper Pelling. Maybe he always had. I pushed myself out of bed and went into the bathroom. I stared into the toilet bowl for a moment, ready to be sick.

Dad knocked on the door. "Honey? You all right?"

"Yes." I choked it out. "Yes. I'm fine."

I thought about David.

"Yes," I said, more to myself now. "Yes. I'm fine."

I took a shower, then combed out my hair. It was easier now, being so short, but I noticed the roots coming in. My natural color clashed with the black dye job. Time to pick up some more hair coloring. Or was that pointless now? I put on the black lace dress I had bought in Bloomington, and then I went back into the room. Dad was kicked back, shoes off, lying on his bed watching television. I asked, "When did you sleep?"

"I haven't yet. I will. Don't worry."

"Are you all right?"

"I'm fine. Why?" He grimaced a bit when he asked.

I shrugged. "Everybody has to sleep. I never see you sleep."

"I'll sleep when I can. I'll be okay. All right?"

To answer, I picked up a doughnut. I went to look out the window but couldn't see anything. "So what's going to happen?"

He laughed. "Nothing. Absolutely nothing."

"Why not?"

"They're trying to outwait me. They know I don't have the money yet, so they're going to wait for me to pick it up."

"I thought that was where you went last night."

"Not exactly."

"What does that mean?"

"I can't say too much, baby." Dad looked around, opened up his arms to gesture at the walls. "This room might be bugged."

I gagged on a bit of doughnut. "What? This room?"

"Sure. Never underestimate your opponent. This is like a chess game. I thought you understood that part. You should. You always were smart. They'll wait a while longer. Maybe put a few screws to us, build up the pressure. But I'll be ready. I've got a gambit."

I nodded. I knew how to play chess, having played many, many games with him before the trouble started. Dad called it all a chess game, but what did chess really have to do with spies and money stashes and crooked cops and running?

Dad said he had a gambit.

Gambit. In chess, a gambit is where a player risks or sacrifices a piece to gain a favorable position in the game. It's a strategic move.

What was Dad's gambit?

What was he risking?

Me?

I couldn't eat anymore. I dropped the rest of the doughnut in the trash and sat down on my bed, watching television with Dad. He just sat there, wide-eyed for a while, and then he said, "Oh. I'm sending you to see somebody."

To say that this came as a supreme shock would be an understatement. "You're doing what?"

"Sending you to see somebody. A friend. Well, not exactly a friend. Somebody who is going to help us."

"Someone here knows us? Who we are?"

"Not exactly. He doesn't ask too many questions."

"Who is he?"

"A photographer. He's going to make us up some passports."

"Forgeries?"

"What can I say, Patty? What can I say?"

Not much, I guess. Dad shook a finger toward the chair where his coat was hanging. "Toss that over, will you?"

I got up and brought it to him.

He went through the pockets, emptying them. Change. His room key. A wadded piece of paper. A thick, stuffed envelope, and a pill bottle. They all fell onto the bed, by his legs.

I was watching the pill bottle. Red with a white label. A prescription of some sort. Dad was saying, "Call yourself a cab. I want you to —"

"What are those?"

"Huh? What?" He blinked at me.

I reached for the pills. "These —"

"Don't." He snatched them up and placed them in the nightstand drawer with the gun and clip. He looked away from me.

I bit my lip. "What are they?"

He sighed. "It's like you said, Patty. Medicine to help me stay awake."

"So what's next?"

"Next?" He turned back to me.

"Yeah, next?" I wrapped my arms around myself and squeezed. "What happens tomorrow? Will you need medicine to help you sleep? Where does all this end?"

"It ends when it ends, Patty."

"How far is all this going to go?"

"Patty . . ."

"Are you going to die?"

"Listen to me."

"You don't answer my questions," I said. "Answer me just this one question: Are you going to die?"

"Not today."

I blinked. What could I say to that?

He waited. "Are you ready now?"

I didn't say anything. He took that for an answer and pulled open the thick envelope. "I want you to take this."

I looked, and almost stepped back. "I thought you said —"

"Stop thinking about everything I say and just listen. I need you to go ahead to Falco's. Get him started. I'll be there later in the day."

"What?" I couldn't seem to find anything to do with my hands. They just hung there.

"Falco is the man's name. The photographer."

"And what am I supposed to do?"

"Take this money with you." He handed me some bills — a lot of them. I asked, "How much is here?"

"Five thousand dollars."

"What?"

"I want you to count out ten hundreds right now."

"How much?"

"One thousand."

I had never seen so much money before in my life, except on television. All of it was in hundred dollar bills. I pulled out eleven and stuffed one back. "Okay."

Dad thought a moment. "Take five hundred and put it in your purse."

"*What?*"

"Put five hundred in your purse. Take the other five hundred and hide it someplace on you, but not in your purse. Never keep all your eggs in one basket."

"The thousand is for me?"

"Yes. Emergency expenses. Just in case."

"In case of what?"

Dad didn't say anything.

"Sorry. So where should I keep the second five hundred?"

"Anywhere. In your shoe. Your bra. Your pocket. Just not in your purse."

"Where does the rest of the money go?"

"Give it to Mr. Falco."

"Four thousand dollars for passports?"

"And other considerations."

I nodded again. "Why aren't you coming with me?"

"I'll catch up. There are things I need to do, and it'll take Falco some time. I want to get him started on you right away."

This was beginning to sound very twisted. It worried me, but I didn't say anything. Instead I asked, "Where am I going?"

"I'll tell the cab driver. Take your stuff."

I did. Twenty minutes after I called, a taxi arrived. Dad explained to the driver about a store on Southern Street in town. Falco's Photographic Supply. The driver nodded; he knew where it was. Dad gave me a twenty to pay the fare with, and I left him standing there, watching me with cool eyes.

I was probably imagining it, but I felt the cabbie was looking at me in his rearview mirror the entire ride. He didn't talk to me at all, except to announce the fare when we stopped in front of Falco's. It was a slightly seedy shop in a section of San Bavispe where I'd never been before. I handed the twenty forward and the driver changed it, saying, "Are you sure this is where you wanted to go?"

I nodded. "Why?"

He pointed to a sign hanging in the door. CLOSED FOR INVENTORY.

I accepted my change, forgetting to tip him. "Yes, this is fine. Thanks." I climbed out of the cab and he pulled slowly away. Maybe I was imagining it, but I felt he was still watching me in the rearview mirror as he slid up the street.

I knocked gently on the door but nobody answered. Curtains were drawn tight. A few people walked by as I stood in the doorway. They gave me odd looks. I knocked harder, making the glass in the door rattle. Finally I heard a shuffling noise inside. A hand moved the CLOSED sign for just an instant and an eye peered out. One eye.

There was a momentary fumbling with locks, then the door opened.

"Come."

I stepped into a dim room. The man snapped the door shut behind me and fiddled with the locks again. "In back," he said.

I followed. He was thin, looking almost starved, with a stubble of growth that would probably never pass for a beard. It was the look of someone who shaved twice weekly. Not like Dad's bleached beard, which seemed to grow fuller with each passing day. But the most significant thing about the man was that he had only one eye; his right eye was covered with a black patch. I had never actually seen a person wearing an eyepatch before. I didn't know how to react.

He led me into the back, where the light was better. The floor was tiled and the walls paneled. There were several rusty sinks, a workbench cluttered with paper cuttings and torn foil packages, and a few shallow tubs of stagnant fluids. A heavy, professional-looking camera, a backdrop, and a small stool stood in the corner. The room had no windows.

The man spoke again. He had a faint but noticeable accent which I suppose was German. "I am Kurt Falco," he said. "And who are you?"

"Uh . . . Karen Peterson," I said.

"You are Patricia Pelling."

"What?"

"I too watch television, evil black box that it is." He smiled. "Surely we can afford ourselves the luxury of a little truth. Is it not a rare commodity in today's world?"

I didn't say anything.

He stepped behind the workbench. "Your father's wishes of me are known."

"You're the photographer?"

"I am the artist. A photographer would be of extremely little value to you, Patricia Pelling. A photographer takes pictures with his camera. He prints up glossy photos of small babies and weddings. Occasionally a pretty nude for a magazine. I am in the business of helping people. I take a small moment of our time to emphasize the word *business*. Do you have the required funds?"

"You mean the money?"

He smiled again. A shark's smile. A wolverine's smile. "Yes. The money."

"I have it."

"May I examine it, please?"

I reached into my purse for the envelope and passed it across the bench to him. He ran his finger across its contents, nodded, and put it in a drawer under one of the sinks. "It is good to complete such business quickly. Asking for money always embarrasses me. Do you not find that so?"

I shrugged. "I guess."

"You guess? Yes. You guess correctly. But let us continue, shall we?"

"Yes."

He looked at me sharply, almost harshly. As if he were examining me, about to make a judgment. His manner made me shiver inside. His eye darted back and forth, up and down. For the longest time he said nothing. Then he spoke, his voice flat. "For the documents you require, one sitting but several days' delay. Your father realizes this, of course. Such things do not come quickly. Step back to the backdrop, please."

He went through the business of loading his camera while I settled myself on the stool, my hands in my lap. He was centering the lens on me, and I guess I was fidgeting. "Sit still," he said.

"Sorry."

"Do not smile. Your photograph will be unconvincing if you smile. No one smiles for a passport photo." He continued adjusting the lens.

It was rude, but I was nervous and had to ask. "Is it hard for you to be a photographer?"

He looked up at me and scratched at the strap of his patch. His smile was there again and his cheeks looked gaunt, like you see in movies about prisoners of war. "You find this eyepatch sexy, no?"

My eyes went wide.

"I have a small problem with depth perception, but I am an adequate man with a camera. You will not find my work in *Life* magazine, perhaps. But I earn considerably more with my skills. Although you might not think so to look at my surroundings. Do not move." He uncapped the lens, snapped the shutter twice, then recapped.

"There. Now you will wait just a moment while I develop the film. To ensure we have proper quality. You can wait here, unless you wish to accompany me into the darkroom . . ." He chuckled, leering.

Once again my blood chilled. When he disappeared into a room even farther back into the building, I left. I stumbled my way through the front of the store, scrambled to get the locks off the door, and hit the street.

I didn't run, but I got out of the immediate neighborhood as fast as I could. If Dad was going to Falco's later, fine. I would meet him back at the motel.

I wandered around downtown for a while, totally confused and terrified, wondering what Dad's real plan was. Why was I carrying a thousand dollars with me? Why had I gone by myself for the passport photo? What was Dad doing when he disappeared on me?

I kept thinking about Dad's comparison of the entire thing to a chess game. Maybe it didn't mean anything at all, but maybe it did. I kept thinking of the definition of a gambit.

Was this Dad's gambit?

Was I the pawn he was prepared to sacrifice in order to win the game?

I hated myself for asking those questions, but another part of me kept saying that it wasn't Dad, Doug Meely, in question. It was Casper Pelling, who admitted to me that (a) he had given secrets to someone who was probably a Soviet agent; (b) he would do it again; (c) he had been in prison and had escaped, hurting people in the process; and (d) he might kill to stay free.

He had taught me to use a gun, and now he was taking pills. Was this Dad? Was this the man who waved from the audience during the junior high Christmas pageant?

What were this man's limits? I had always known Dad's moral code. The rules I was brought up under. But that was all gone now. Casper Pelling was definitely not Doug Meely. So the real question was . . . did I still love him?

There it was. Cold. Out in the open.

Did I still love him?

Would I be expected to? Didn't fifteen years of lies kill that? Wasn't that love null and void?

I was bitter. For a second I thought of turning him in, and the thought scared me. But I had to wonder: Did I still love him?

I didn't know. Not for sure.

All I knew was that I felt very much alone. And afraid. I thought again about where I was going next, about the planned afternoon with David Borrego. Should I be going all out to *save myself?*

How would I do that?

I was approaching the San Bavispe Bank. It was a little after one in the afternoon. Still over two hours before I could meet David at the Dairy Queen for whatever else this day entailed. On an impulse I went into the bank and got a ten-dollar roll of quarters with the change from the ride that morning. I wasn't even thinking about the thousand dollars I was carrying. Then I walked down the street to a phone booth. It was an old-fashioned booth with a folding door for privacy.

I broke open the roll of coins and dialed the number. My hands were shaking, but I managed. A computer voice popped on and requested I deposit my money. I fed some coins in. It started to ring.

After four rings Mom answered. Kimmers' mother. "Hello?"

I had to search for my voice. "Is . . . is Kimmers around?"

"She's in school. Who is this?"

"It's . . . Mom, it's me. Patty."

"Oh my . . ." Her voice trailed off.

"Hello?"

She came back strong. "Patty? Are you all right? Where are you?"

"I . . ." Swallowing once more I said, "I can't say where. I'm okay."

"Is your dad with you?"

"Yes. He's okay."

"Has he hurt you?"

"What? No. Why would he?"

"The news . . ."

"A lot of what they're saying isn't true, Mom. It can't be."

"I don't know, Patty. I think you're in bad trouble. I want to help if I can . . ."

"Mom, I'm so scared."

"I know."

"Is Kimmers okay?"

"She's fine. Listen, honey, there has to be a way for you to come home."

"No. This is too big. I'm stuck."

"Patty . . ."

Suddenly, standing there in the phone booth, I got very scared. I don't know why. "Mom, I have to go —"

Then it happened.

There was a click on the line and a new voice cut

in. Heavy and male. "Patty, this is Ray Munroe of the FBI. Please don't hang up."

My blood was ice. My hands were stone.

"Patty, I just want you to take a breath and relax. I want you to answer a question for me. One question. You can do that, can't you?"

I swallowed.

"Are you in fact okay? Are you traveling of your own free will?"

"What?"

"There are some things that you don't know about your father, Patty. I just want you to relax a minute and talk to me. Can you do that?"

"Talk about what?"

"There are some things you don't know —"

I slapped the phone down. They were tracing the call.

I didn't know how far they had gotten.

TWELVE

The license bureau was crowded when we got there about three-thirty: I counted four different lines. A big sign proclaimed this to be a tiny spot in the great hierarchy of the California Department of Motor Vehicles. David Borrego and I stood behind a woman with red hair tied in a net. She coughed a lot. David was wearing a blue T-shirt beneath his jacket and boots with his jeans. His hair was fluffing out now that he'd taken off his helmet. He had a bandage on his left hand.

"Did you do that with your bike?"

"What?"

"Did you fall?"

"No, no." He waved the hand. "Fang bit me yesterday."

"Your dog?"

"My tarantula."

"Your *what*?"

"Tarantula. They're these big, hairy spiders—"

"I know what a tarantula is."

"So why did you ask?" He grinned.

"Why do you have a tarantula?"

"Because they're these big, hairy spiders—"

"*Please.*"

"Sorry."

I shuddered at the very thought. But I still wondered why he would keep a big, hairy spider. "Is it a pet?"

"Yeah. They make great pets. Friendly—"

"I can see."

"No, this was just a thing."

"Was it a painful thing?"

"Well, yeah. It swells. You know."

"What it's like to be bitten by a tarantula? No, I didn't know. I thought you died."

He felt his own chest. Poked himself in the cheek. "Nope. Guess not."

"Funny."

"So have you been studying?"

"What?"

He looked around. "For the test."

"What test?"

"What test?" He blinked at me. "For the *driver's test.* You didn't think you just walked in and they gave you a license, did you?"

"Actually, I did." I swallowed. The line moved forward a bit. "Is the test hard?"

"Outrageous. I failed three times."

"You did?"

"Well, I don't count the first time. That was practice, you know?"

My stomach churned. "You failed the test *four* times?"

"Sort of, yeah."

"*Sort of?*"

He smiled at me.

"You're lying to me, aren't you, you little twerp?"

"Would a man with a tarantula wound lie to you?"

"At every available opportunity."

"Right. I guess he would." He kept smiling.

I punched him.

It wasn't a very hard punch; I just laid it into his shoulder. He wasn't knocked unconscious or anything. Actually, all he did was laugh. So did I — it felt good getting into a little harmless weirdness. As opposed to the real life weirdness. I was enjoying every moment. About now Dad would be at Falco's. Or was he finished there already? What would he be doing?

Did I care?

David and I were both looking around the place. It was hot and stuffy and people were smoking, despite the PLEASE DON'T SMOKE demands in English, Spanish, and international symbolism. David said, "Did I ever tell you what an exciting date you are, Karen Peterson?"

"Frequently."

"Well, let me re-emphasize it. This is awesome."

"Thanks."

"What do you do on prom night? Apply for jobs?"

I groaned. "So what do you want from me? Trading stamps?"

"Sure. How many books to get me a new helmet?"

"What's wrong with the one you have?"

"It's not dramatic enough. I need something with lightning bolts or something. Something to attract the girls."

"You're weird."

"Only because you're contagious."

I was next.

The coughing lady moved aside and I stepped up. There was a geek behind the counter who looked unhappy in his work, and I anticipated trouble. His nameplate said WARREN KEATING and he wore big horn-rimmed glasses. He had long, thin fingers. "Next!" he half yelped.

I switched the charm to full power, but it still felt weak. "Hi, there."

He blinked, not looking too impressed.

I made an instant decision. Where I was getting these sick ideas was beyond me, but it seemed the thing to do. Drawing myself up to full height, which admittedly isn't much, I played mock, friendly annoyance to the hilt. "Well, Warren Keating, I cannot believe you. . . ."

He looked instantly embarrassed. I thought he was the type to panic. He looked a lot like Carl Rudnick, a guy from my algebra class. Correction. A guy from the algebra class I used to be in. "Uh . . . can I help you?" he asked.

I laid it on thick. "You don't remember?"

"Remember?"

"I know your momma."

"Mom?"

"You don't *remember* me?"

"Well, uh, sort of . . ."

I thought so.

I laughed, smiling some more. "Well, I finally decided to do what you were saying."

"Uh . . ." Warren Keating looked around a bit, confused. The question was whether he would admit to not remembering me or pretend to *sort of* remember.

I pretended to remind him. No. That's not right. I *lied* to him. "You said there was no reason not to go ahead and get a driver's license. Even if I don't have a car."

"Uh . . . right." He swallowed and nodded.

"So here I am." I pushed my birth certificate forward. Here went nothing. "So when is your momma going to let you out nights?"

"Uh . . . whenever, I guess." He looked at the photocopy. "This isn't a certified copy . . ."

"What?"

"You need the county seal impressed on this document. This is just a photocopy. It doesn't really mean anything."

"It doesn't?"

"Well, not really. No."

"But you know me. Right?"

Tick, tick, tick . . .

He cleared his throat. "Yeah. Sort of, I guess."

I smiled wider. "Well. Isn't there any way you could bend just a little? I know you shouldn't . . ."

"I —"

"Please?"

He weakened. "You really should get a certified copy. . . ."

"Yeah."

"But . . . for now I guess . . ."

"Yeah."

He looked around, folding the paper back up and returning it to me. "Jeez, just don't tell my boss."

"Cross my heart and hope to die."

He squirmed a bit but smiled back. "Come on over for the eye exam."

I noticed he had marked on my application that I was positively identified as Karen Millicent Peterson.

Now all I had to do was pass the test.

The written part was no problem. I only missed two questions, and I passed. Warren Keating gave me a number and told me to wait until it was called. David, who hadn't said anything throughout all of this, followed me. Sat down next to me. Finally asked, "So what was all that?"

I put a finger to my lips to quiet him.

He looked around. "Is that how they do things in New Zealand?"

"Yeah. Sort of."

"What does 'sort of' mean?"

I turned to him. "It's like when you ride your motorcycle on the sidewalk. Everybody screams for your head, but they never see the van that put you there. Right?"

He thought about it and didn't say anything.

My number was called at 4:45. I followed the examiner out to the state vehicle. He was a short man, fat, in an old, rumpled brown suit. He fastened his seat belt and I did the same. It occurred to me then that I was still only fifteen and had only driven a car five times before, and not for very long. The one thing I had going for me was the fact that the car had an automatic transmission. No clutch. "You may start the engine when you're ready," he said.

David was standing there waiting. He waved.

I turned the key. The car rattled to life. It was in pretty bad shape.

"I'm Tom Urich, your driving examiner," he said. He was scribbling on a clipboard and rattling the words off by rote. "Very simply, I will instruct you to drive around the block obeying all pertinent traffic laws. Is that understood?"

"Yes, sir."

"It's a breeze. You'll pass as long as you don't kill anybody."

I laughed. Relaxed some.

"Pull away from the curb," he said.

I did, again amazed at how weird life was getting.

Who would have thought that Patty Meely would take her first driver's test in San Bavispe, California? Under an assumed name, yet. The examiner shocked me by asking, "Are you from Indiana?"

I looked at him, blank. Was he psychic? Did he know who I was?

He gestured with the clipboard. "It's on your application."

"Yeah." I quickly looked back to the road.

"What part?"

I lied. Easily. "Muncie."

"Oh."

"Ever been there?"

"To Indiana? No. I've never been out of California. Turn left here, please."

The test, as he had promised, was a breeze. He took me back inside to finish the paperwork. The bureau closed at five-thirty and was nearly empty. They took my picture with a Polaroid camera on a tripod and ten minutes later presented me with a California driver's license in the name of Karen Millicent Peterson. She was seventeen, almost eighteen. Warren Keating's hands were shaking when I accepted it from him. "What's wrong?" I asked.

"I think I remember you now. Disneyland, right? Last year."

I smiled. "Yeah. That's it."

"I gotta go." He took off toward the back of the office.

I wonder what happened at Disneyland?

189

Outside, David was waiting. "So what now?"

"What do you mean, what now?"

"Do I get to impress you? Or what?"

"What kind of an option is 'or what'?"

"Keeps you guessing."

"So do math tests."

"But you don't go to school."

"Eventually."

He grabbed my arm. "Come on." I climbed onto the bike with him. He had warned me about holding on tight and I warned him again about going too fast. I wrapped my arms around his waist. They felt good there. I leaned into him and he throttled the bike off.

We buzzed down the street. The light was beginning to fade. "Where are we going?" I yelled into his ear.

He shook his head. "Don't yell so loud — I can hear you. We're just going for a ride."

Why not? I leaned in and held tighter.

He never really did anything dangerous, but just being on a motorcycle going fifty miles or so an hour was scary enough. One turn he banked into so far that I was positive we were going to fall. I screamed, but he throttled forward again, and I doubt he heard it. Finally we wound up coasting to a stop at the Dairy Queen. It was after six-thirty; we had been riding for a while. I don't think he wanted to stop. I didn't want to, either. I was yelling though, as a formality. He was laughing as he pulled his helmet off.

"You're a genuine nasty," I said, climbing off the bike.

"A what?"

"A genuine nasty. One of the original few."

"Gee, thanks." He got off the bike himself, asking if I wanted anything. I should have been back at the motel, by now, but I shrugged. Again, why not? He disappeared for a minute and returned with two drinks. I sipped mine and gagged. "Root beer?"

"Nectar of the gods." He slurped his, sitting at a table near his bike. It was the same table I had been sitting at that day when we first talked.

I was looking at his bike. "What kind of a motorcycle is that?"

"Well, there's big ones, and then there's small ones. Stop me if I get too technical. That there is a *medium*-size one."

"Funny." I grimaced, taking another sip of the root beer. "Does your mother know you terrify young girls with that thing?"

His smile twitched a bit. "No."

"What does she think about this thing?"

He looked blank a second. "Well, actually, she's dead."

"What?" I held my breath, thinking he was kidding.

He wasn't. "Last year. Cancer."

"I'm sorry."

"Don't be."

"No. Really. I know how stupid that sounds. My mom's gone too. I know how it hurts."

He didn't say anything.

"I don't even remember my mom. It was so long ago. Sometimes I think I do, but it could be anybody. You know?"

"Yeah."

I tried to brighten things up. I banged on his helmet. "So is this what you're going to do with your life? Is that it?"

"What?"

"Do you want to be a stunt man or something?"

"Oh, all that." He made a face. "No. I'm going to be a fish."

"A what?"

"An oceanographer."

"How's that?"

He grinned. "Living on a boat. Studying the sea. The fish, sharks, whales. All the creatures. I want to know everything there is to know about the ocean."

"Sounds like a challenge."

"Sure."

"How long does something like that take?"

"My whole life, I hope."

"Is there much money in that? In the ocean?"

"Well, fish don't carry wallets, but —"

"You know what I mean."

He opened his arms, an easy gesture. "Just so long as I survive I'll be happy."

"Is that all you want to do? Survive? Doesn't anybody want to *live* anymore?"

"What do you mean, live? You mean big houses, traveling, all of that?"

"Yeah. Why not?"

"A lot of trouble."

"What's wrong with trouble?"

"Oh — and you like trouble?"

"I'm beginning to," I said. What did that mean? I wondered.

He laughed. "Okay, smart guy. So what are you going to do?"

"I'm going to get out there and cause some trouble."

"No, really."

I went blank. "I don't know."

"You don't know?"

"I knew a minute ago. I really did. I just can't remember now. . . ."

He looked at me, shaking his head slowly. "So I guess you just plan to follow in your dad's footsteps?"

I went cold again. "*What?*"

"Well, I figured with him being rich and all . . ."

"Who said he was rich?"

"Seems like it."

"Does it?"

David laughed again. "You answer a lot of questions with questions. You even answer a lot of answers with questions."

"Do I?" I was grinning, and *he* hit *me* in the

shoulder this time. I asked, "What's your school like?"

He couldn't think of an answer, I guess. He asked, "What's any school like?"

"I could tell you stories—"

"Okay."

"Okay? Tell you stories?"

"Yeah."

I thought a second. About Kimmers. About the life that didn't exist anymore.

"Go ahead," David said. "I'm listening."

I looked at him, stalling some. "You're not listening—you're looking."

"What's the difference?"

"The difference is that you look with your eyes and you listen with your ears. You remember your ears? They're those big, flappy things hiding under your hair."

"Can't I look and listen all at once?"

"I don't think you can."

"Let me try. Tell me a story."

"No." I looked away. "No point getting into any of that."

"What?" He blinked. "No point getting into any of what?"

I didn't say anything.

"Mystery," said David. "You want everything about you to be a mystery, don't you? Why?"

"It keeps things exciting. Doesn't it?"

"I'm going to find out some day."

"Maybe. Maybe you won't like what you find out."

David just looked at me. Then he tilted his head a bit. "Listen," he said.

"What?"

"I know a secret."

I felt almost cold again. "What?"

"A secret. I know a secret."

"And?"

He leaned in to whisper. "The secret is this: There is no secret."

I looked at him, at his eyes. Into them. "I know."

He kissed me.

Just for a second, we only touched lips for a second, but he didn't pull back. I didn't either. We just stayed there, about a millimeter apart, for the longest time. I wasn't absolutely sure that I was breathing. When I was, I pulled back some. I tried to smirk. "Some secret."

"You won't catch me telling anyone." He smiled.

I waited. Then I had to smile back.

David just took a breath. "You confuse me."

"That's intentional."

"Is it?"

I opened my arms out wide. "It's a big, lost world out there. Everyone is confused by it. Don't sit around on your motorcycle expecting answers. There are too many mountains to climb and too few gurus worth the effort. Just pay your check before you leave. I have to go."

"Wait."

195

I did, but just for a moment.

He picked up his helmet. "Can I have your phone number?"

"No." That was easy.

"But . . ."

"But what?"

He sighed. "But you're the weirdest girl I ever met."

I hesitated. "You already said that."

"I know. I'm waiting for it to mean something."

"It meant something. A long time ago."

"So why can't I call?"

"I'll explain it later. Okay?"

"I want to see you. A lot."

"Please."

"Karen . . ."

"I have to go." I didn't want to leave, but I didn't like where all this was heading. Correction: I liked where it was heading, but it scared me.

"Karen . . ."

The name stopped me; I don't know why. It wasn't my name. Was it? I turned. "Are you still jumping Saturday?"

He nodded.

"Maybe I'll come watch."

"Really?"

"Yeah. Maybe. If you promise not to kill yourself."

"I promise."

I turned to walk.

"Hey!"

"Hey, what?"

"Are you sure I can't just give you a ride home?"

I shook my head. "My dad wouldn't like that."

"Seriously?"

"Seriously."

I started walking again. As before, he called after me. "You're beautiful, Karen Peterson!" This time I didn't shudder.

Why should I?

I *was* Karen Peterson. I had a California driver's license to prove it. Wasn't that a start? A beginning? I walked back up toward the Cactus Place, feeling for once very happy with my spot in the world.

Ten minutes later I was kidnapped.

THIRTEEN

Dad told me a lot of things between Wednesday and Friday. About South America. About our escape plan. He explained how our first stop would have to be Brazil or Argentina, but from there we could easily immigrate to Australia or New Zealand.

I didn't tell Dad anything.

I didn't tell him about how I had been kidnapped, taken right off the street by three sinister creeps in a blue Ford. When I came home, shaken, he knew something was up.

"Patty, what happened?"

"Nothing." I sat down, carefully, in front of the television.

He didn't believe me. "I don't think it's nothing."

I turned on him, tears on my face. "I met a guy. Okay?"

"A guy?"

"Yeah." Now the tears were really flowing.

Dad frowned. "And that makes you cry?"

"I know I'm never going to see him again. Okay?"

Dad bit his lower lip, but he didn't know what to say. Finally he went back to his paper.

I couldn't tell him anything about the kidnapping. Not then. They told me they would kill me if I did, and I believed them. I didn't mention chess, either, or gambits or Mr. Falco or my new driver's license or anything. Instead, on Friday when Dad went out I took the gun and his pills outside and buried them in the sand. I didn't mark the location; I didn't want them found again. Then I went back to the room.

Dad got back around four. He was in the room for about fifteen minutes before he opened the drawer. He looked over at me, parked by the television.

His eyes met mine. "Where is it?"

"Gone."

"Patty . . ."

"I got rid of the pills, too. Which are you missing the most?"

"Patty . . ."

I turned to the television. "It's all starting to end. Can't you feel it? It's in the air. But it can't end like that. Pills, the gun — either one will get you killed."

"Patty, in just a little while we'll —"

"There is no while longer!" I got up. "It's ending. It is all ending!" I was in tears again, shaking.

Dad went pale. "Oh, my God. What happened?"

"I . . . I can't tell you."

"What?"

I just looked around the room. Couldn't speak.

Dad got mad. He left the room, and I thought he was angry at me until he returned with a new set of room keys. "Come on," he said. Moving around quickly, he stuffed things into our bags. I was slow, stumbling, but I helped. "Grab your shoes," he said. I did.

We moved from room 19 to room 32.

"Okay." Dad tossed the bags onto a bed. He closed the door and grabbed me by the shoulders. Looking into my eyes, he said, "They couldn't possibly have bugged every room in this motel. Understand? I told them which room I wanted this time — they didn't force thirty-two on me. Now what's happened? What are you afraid of?"

I blubbered some. "A . . . a man with white hair. Pink eyes."

"An albino?"

I didn't know. "He said the money was his. You stole it from him."

Dad looked grim. "And?"

"They took me in a car. Said they'd kill me if I said anything to you. They said they would know if I did."

Dad just nodded.

"I don't want this anymore. I don't want you to get hurt. That's why I hid the gun. The pills."

"I know."

"He said you were careless. He said there were too many people involved, and he couldn't wait anymore. They wanted to know where the money was."

"And you didn't know."

I nodded. "I didn't know."

"And they believed you?"

"The white-haired man said, '*Find out.*'"

"Which means they'll come for you again."

I shivered.

Dad seethed. "Yeah. I know this guy. That's his style all right."

I grabbed his arm. "Daddy, let's just leave. We can't get the money anyway. Let's just go. Now. Tonight."

He shook his head. "That wouldn't work now. We've waited too long. They'd just grab us and we'd wind up dead and buried out in the desert. No, we have to confront these vultures. Here."

"Daddy, no . . ." I was still crying.

He patted my hand and looked confident. "Hey, what's to worry? This is almost the moment. My whole life — or at least the last twenty years — has been leading up to this. We're going to get a boat, okay? Sail that sloop around the world."

"If something goes wrong . . ."

Dad didn't say anything. Just held my arm a little tighter.

I blurted it: "If something goes wrong, we'll meet. Okay?"

"We can't. Remember?"

"No. We can meet a year from now."

"What?"

"Yeah." I was thinking out loud. "If we get separated and have to go our own ways, we'll meet in a secret place. In a year. Or any year after that. Every year at the same place, on the same day."

Dad started to shake his head.

"Promise me."

"Okay," he said. "Where?"

I told him.

He didn't smile. He just nodded. Then he pulled away from me. "Stay packed. I'll be back as soon as I can."

I was scared — more than scared. I was about to be alone. For real. "Where are you going?"

"To see Skyler. The man with the white hair."

I freaked. I hate to say it, but I did. It was all building up. "No! You can't! He's crazy! He's dangerous!"

"No." Dad stood in the doorway. "I'm the one who's crazy. I'm the one who's dangerous."

He pulled the door shut behind him. And he never came back.

I fell apart.

It was a scramble, and I didn't know which way to turn or run. I reached for my bag, ripped open the zipper, and pushed into it. One of the first things I pulled out was my jacket — the old one which I had last worn in Bloomington. The pockets were stuffed with things, and I took a second to empty them.

My past life spilled out onto the bed.

Past life. How long ago? Really? Less than three weeks?

How far had I broken down since then?

The stuff in my pockets had been recovered from Helker. Agent Helker? FBI? What was he really? I had filled my pockets at the Gizzales' house, just before sneaking out the window.

I thought about Mr. Wise, the cat. I wondered how he was.

The stuff on the bed all looked so bizarre. So foreign.

A comb, a pocketbook, a pen, and a diary.

My twice-photocopied, well-distributed diary.

I flipped slowly through the pages, as if I was ashamed of what was inside. Afraid, maybe. But it wasn't even me. It was the diary of some girl named Patrica Meely. Who was she?

I thought about Dad, the way he had looked before he left. *"I'm the one who's crazy,"* he'd said. Maybe that was true, too. Maybe everything was true. Maybe it was possible to be Casper Pelling, Lou Peterson, and Doug Meely at the same time. Who was I to say?

Do we ever really tread new ground? I wondered. Or is this all there is: To become lost in the familiar?

Was I, now, just the shadow of someone nobody had seen in a long, long time?

I got up and looked at myself in the mirror. Makeup, short black hair, hard look. I didn't recognize the face.

I went back and read some of the diary, but stopped at a certain page:

> "Did you know," Mark asked today, "that ice cream has no bones?"

Mark? Who was that?

> "It's so fascinating," he said, "to consider all the implications of life."
> "Which are?" I wondered.
> "What would an ice cream skeleton look like?"
> Mark is so weird, but . . . All these strange things, all the phone calls, and still he hasn't asked me out. Does he want me to ask him? I could I guess. Why not? I've heard that outgoing people are really shy on the inside. Maybe that's true, but it seems impossible with him. I asked him why he didn't go to the movie Saturday, like he said he was going to. I didn't tell him Kimmers and I were there, waiting. He asked, "What if I had gone?"
> "What?"
> "What if I had been there?"
> I hate questions like that. I said, "What if worms had machine guns?"
> This got him. "What?"
> I smiled. "If worms had machine guns, birds wouldn't bother them."

And that was where I stopped reading the diary.

I used to *what if?* my life all the time, rewriting things in my head. Not anymore. Not even under these circumstances. I learned that lesson the hard way, in the ninth grade.

204

It was almost eleven o'clock, and I was bundled in a corner of my bed, using the pillows and blankets as insulation. I was waiting for Dad to get back, wondering if he would, when the door jiggled and popped open. I watched.

The first guy through the door had a gun. Long and thick and ready. It was Marshal Mitch — Mitch Doonegan, I remembered. The United States marshal who had driven me to the Gizzales' that day and bought me the cheeseburger. I tried to jump, but I didn't have the energy. No, scratch that. I just didn't feel like it.

Now. Now it was ending.

Marshal Rogers followed him in. He was wearing the same brown jacket and tie and the same unhappy look. I remembered guessing he was over fifty. He looked older than that. I don't know if it was a frown or what, but he nodded. "Patty."

I didn't move.

"I know he's not here, Patty. So I don't want you to be scared. Okay?"

I was still watching Marshal Mitch, standing casually with his gun.

Rogers turned to him, looking suddenly annoyed. "Mitch, don't be so dramatic. It's not necessary. Put it away."

Mitch did. He jammed his hands in the pockets of his slacks, looking, believe it or not, embarrassed.

Rogers scratched his nose and stepped forward. "I'm gonna sit down. Is that okay?"

I still had blankets pulled up to my neck. I nodded.

Rogers moved the chair a bit and settled into it. He cupped his hands. "Like I said, Patty, I don't want you to get scared."

I didn't say anything. Couldn't yet.

Rogers said, "I'm not here to take you to jail. Not even your dad. Can you believe me on that?"

A thought was racing through my head, but it didn't connect. I just nodded.

Rogers looked around. "Talking's dry work. You want something to drink? Mitch, go on out to that soda machine and get us some cold drinks. Okay?"

Mitch backed out of the room. Rogers leaned forward again. "Listen to me, Patty."

I did.

"I know all about the money," he said. "I have for a long time. Your daddy's a brilliant man, but he's not so smart as he thinks. Except for one thing, of course. He was smart enough to go back for you. You're a treasure."

I waited.

"There's something you should know, but I guess maybe you already figured part of it out. Bob — Bob Helker, you remember him — he thinks he's the greatest thing since sliced bread and the toaster. Well, he's sort of stupid. I could have taken your father anytime after 1973. But I figured, you know, why do it? He was living straight, on top of things. And as for the money, well . . . I had years to go before retirement. It could all wait. I figured I'd just wait it all out, then drop by the house one afternoon. For a talk. You know?"

I caught on then. "You mean for blackmail."

"Sharing. He doesn't need all that money and you know it. Besides, seems to me he would be willing to pay a small price for peace of mind. Probably still would. Anyway, that isn't important anymore."

"Why not?"

"It's like this. One day, Bright-eyes Bob cuts himself in, hot on the chase. Special agent from Washington. Terrific, right? Bob's been reading old files, doing some odd research. He's got a theory now that maybe Casper Pelling is hiding out in northern Indiana somewhere and he wants to check it out. I couldn't exactly discourage him — how would that look? But I didn't go out of my way to help, either. Not until things got too far along to stop."

Rogers looked very, very sad. "I didn't like that thing that went on down at your school. It was stupid and dangerous and unnecessary. We could have taken him very quietly, at work, anywhere. It didn't have to be like that — you didn't have to see it. I'm sorry. But that was Bob all along, Bright-eyes Bob."

"I thought he was crooked."

"What?"

I shuffled myself up in the blankets. "I thought Helker was crooked. I thought that was why he was chasing us."

"No." Rogers shook his head. "Bright-eyes Bob is just another hero trying to make a name for himself."

"And what about you?"

"I don't believe in heroes anymore." Rogers swallowed.

The door opened. Doonegan came in with three sodas. One was an orange drink, which he kept, the other two were colas. He gave one to me.

Rogers said, "I've got a daughter your age. I told you that, right? I've got family to take care of. You know?"

"You guys want the money."

"We're not greedy. We're not like those other wolverines — we know that there's plenty to go around. I've got enough status to keep these people off your back long enough for you to get away. Out of the country. I'm talking about a deal now. Heck, I'm the one who made it possible for your dad to walk away on the Interstate. It wasn't an accident that Mitch here was on the detail."

Mitch just sort of smiled. "I got a letter of reprimand for that."

"Which ought to be worth something," said Rogers. "Listen, we're not bad guys." It was almost like he was apologizing to me. "A bad guy would leave you and your father in a swamp somewhere. I don't care about any of that. But it's all coming together tonight. It's all ending *tonight*. I pulled the right cords, and the cops have closed out a lot of the bad guys. But that can't last. Either we all settle up tonight, or I have to play it straight and take you both in. Otherwise you'll end up dead, and I don't want that."

I waited. Just looking. Finally I asked a question. "Isn't anyone who they're supposed to be anymore? I thought you were a good guy."

"What's a good guy?"

I thought about it. "A good guy is somebody who doesn't have to wear a mask all the time. Somebody who doesn't have to lie."

"Oh. And what about you?"

I didn't answer.

Rogers gestured. "Why don't you go look in the mirror, Patty?" His voice was soft. "What do you see in there? Patty Meely ready to go to trig class? Or somebody else?"

He sighed. "We all wear masks, Patty."

I guessed he was right. I tried to distract him some by telling him about Skyler, the white-haired man, and Longhair, who followed me. He just said, "Don't worry about all that. Everything winds down tonight. I'm sorry, but that's the way it is. Now, I need to know this. Really. Where's your father?"

I thought a second. I was staying cool, since calmness seemed to be my only ally, but I was also disgusted with myself. I was sick of being the victim all the time, being passive, being just someone else's instrument. I could survive. I knew that. I proved that with Helker and by getting the driver's license. I decided to see if I could prove it to myself. "It's not supposed to end tonight," I said. "It's supposed to end tomorrow."

Rogers looked interested. "How is that?"

"We don't get hurt? We get to leave?"

"Yes. I said that."

I took a breath. "Tomorrow. At the road and track show. I'm supposed to meet him there, and then we're leaving."

Rogers hesitated, suspicious. "He's not coming back here tonight?"

"No."

"How are you guys leaving tomorrow?"

"I don't know. I'm just supposed to be there."

Rogers sighed again. "Okay, here's a thought. We'll wait here tonight. If your dad doesn't come back, then . . . we'll all go to the road and track show. Together."

I didn't say anything else.

FOURTEEN

Saturday morning. Rogers and Mitch slowed their car to a halt outside the fairgrounds stadium. The gravel parking lot was crowded with vehicles of all descriptions, and people were shuffling in and out of the stadium. Booths were set up, peddling trinkets and books and models and food and drink. Rogers looked over his seat to me in the back. His eyes were red; he and Mitch looked ragged from lack of sleep. I didn't feel much better; I had dozed on occasion, but every noise and creak brought me back, terrified it might be Dad and then disappointed when it wasn't. All in all, though, my nerves had calmed some. I guess the term is *burned out*.

Rogers said, "You go ahead in. We'll be close by."

I nodded. "Is that supposed to be a threat? Or a comfort?"

"I wish this didn't have to be so hard."

"You could leave us alone."

He ignored that, saying instead, "When the time comes, try to stay calm. It'll be easier on everybody."

I didn't want to reply to that, but I nodded. Rogers unlocked my door for me and I got out. I bought a gate pass with the ten dollars he had given me — saving my own money — and went into the arena.

Lightheaded. That's how I felt. I had absolutely no idea what I was doing. Dad wasn't going to be within light-years of this place, but I knew it was crawling with people looking for him. Rogers and Mitch couldn't be the only ones. Well, let them look, I thought. Let them follow me all day. Let it end here, finally. The only thing I wanted to do was see David Borrego again.

The two men came up from behind and snagged me very professionally. If you weren't watching for it, you might never have noticed. I lost a breath as they took me almost gently by the arms and started carrying me down the corridor of the stadium. I knew I should be terrified, but I was exhausted and the whole thing seemed hilarious to me: I was being kidnapped on an almost daily basis. But these guys were not graysuits, and it wasn't Helker or Rogers or Mitch.

It was Longhair. And another man with a totally flat nose, flaring nostrils, and wide lips. They both wore black sunglasses and dark blue suits with long ties. What now? CIA? KGB? They could be from Mars for all I knew. I almost giggled. Had Dad been selling secrets to Mars?

I asked, "Who are you guys? Just so I can tell what day it is. If it's Tuesday, you must be FBI."

"Just be quiet."

"Come on, you gotta give me a hint."

Longhair grunted. "Shut your mouth or die right here. Just like in the movies, Patty Pelling. Only it'll just be once, and for a long, long time."

I swallowed, my heart skipping a beat. This could be serious. I looked around, or tried to. They were being kind of rough. Where were Rogers and Mitch, now that I needed them? So much for being close by. I looked at Longhair and asked, "Have you got my dad, too?"

"Don't speak."

I resisted their pull. "Where are you taking me?"

"Be quiet."

"Why? I'll have to go to the principal's office?"

They said nothing.

"I could scream very loudly now. Lots of people here."

One of them whispered, "If you scream, you die. In the same breath."

The other said, "Just like in the movies."

I couldn't see which said which. It didn't matter. Longhair smiled through broken teeth. "Silence is golden."

I could see he was serious. He would kill me.

"This way." He tugged at my arm.

I had no options.

They led me down the corridor, toward a sign:

THIS WAY TO PARKING AREA. They had just about dragged me there when David appeared out of nowhere, smiling, glad to see me. He didn't seem to notice the two men hurrying me along. "Hey, Karen!"

My escorts were startled. I jerked away and rushed around some people to where David was standing.

David looked shocked to see me coming at him like that. He was grinning, though, until Flatnose reached out to grab me. I snapped back, swinging my purse into his face.

The brick I had been carrying inside it since Wednesday, after the first kidnapping, helped.

It smashed hard into his face. There was a sick sound and it made his nose just a little bit flatter. He started to crumple.

Longhair started grappling for me, but I was fighting. He snatched the purse away and it fell with a clunk. Blood was gushing from Flatnose as he struggled to stand. I twisted from Longhair and started to run again. David seemed boggled by what he saw, but his reflexes were fast. He jammed out a foot. I got by, but Longhair tripped and landed on his face. David hurried after me. He was yelling. "Karen! Hey, wait!"

I couldn't wait. I wanted to stop for him but I knew he couldn't save me. I had to do that myself. My heart was pounding. I ran down a passageway that led to the track. I could hear motors rumbling and gunning out there, and the crowd. A red rope blocked my path, and I started to scramble under it. A hand grabbed my shoulder.

I spun around to punch, but it was David. He jumped back. "Hey! You'll get killed out there! It's the demolition derby!"

I looked. Cars were colliding with each other in a sort of playful way. The crowd loved it. The old stock cars roared by, only yards in front of us.

Down at the end of the passageway, behind David, Longhair appeared.

"Doesn't matter!" I yelled, grabbing David. I pulled him beneath the rope with me. "Come on! Run!"

He did, yelling, "What's happening?"

"They're trying to kill me!"

"What?"

"David, please!"

He was running with me now, down the track's sideline. He must have seen something in my eyes because he didn't hesitate. He jerked ahead and pulled me by the hand toward the greasy mechanics' pits.

"Hey, Dave!" somebody yelled. "Aren't you set up yet?"

Further ahead, scrambling down a wall, I saw Mitch Doonegan. Running at us now. Behind, Longhair charged out of the tunnel onto the track sidelines.

David ignored the people shouting at him. We were in his pit, where the crew was waiting. I noticed that somebody had painted BORREGO in flaming red letters on the gas tank of his motorcycle. David was staring behind us. The look in his eyes made me turn as well.

Both Longhair and the bleeding Flatnose were moving steadily toward us. Steadily. Trying not to attract too much attention.

David made his decision right away. "Get on."

"What?"

"The bike. Get on the bike."

He had already climbed on and was pulling at me. A thin man with a mustache leaped up, but David said, "Later, Roy!"

He jumped only once, kick-starting the engine. He looked at me again. "Come on, Karen!"

Longhair and Flatnose were closer now. Ahead of us, Mitch Doonegan was moving closer. I couldn't see where Marshal Rogers was. I hopped on the bike. No sooner had I grabbed hold of David then we were throttling away. Fast. My heart skipped a beat and I closed my eyes for a moment but then had to open them. We almost wiped out right away because David had to turn around quickly to avoid a dead end in the pit alley. He leaned back, gunned the engine again, and raced past Longhair and Flatnose as they turned and started to trot after us.

We were much faster, of course, and left them in a puff of rising dust.

David charged the bike across the track and I almost died right then and there. Literally. The stadium crowd yelped in excitement as we crossed the path of the oncoming demolition derby cars. I closed my eyes again until I felt the bump of the infield. We were racing across the center of the track, passing among people who shouted and screamed at us. The engine whined, roared, and sputtered. All David said was "Hang on!"

He crossed the track again on the other side and roared out of the stadium and away from the fairgrounds. He never looked back, but I did. Nobody was following. It would have been very difficult for them to, anyway.

The fairgrounds were out in the middle of nowhere, and David drove even deeper into the boonies. He finally stopped just long enough to ask, "Who were those guys?"

"I don't know."

He throttled again, roaring us away. We ended up on high ground: a grassy bluff overlooking what was mostly desert, or at least the closest thing to a desert I had ever seen. David parked the bike and switched off the engine. We had been riding for almost an hour. He climbed off. "It's okay," he said. "We can see for miles. Nobody will sneak up."

He was right. As long as it was daylight, we could not be sneaked up on. It would be difficult even in the dark.

David sat down in the grass. He unzipped his jacket. He looked hot. I didn't sit; I just stood, gazing into space. I was still shaking.

David said, "I suppose I shouldn't ask . . ."

I shrugged. "I don't know."

"I do. You're the girl on television. I understand it all now. All the weirdness before. Jeez, this is crazy. Your dad is that escaped spy. Isn't he?"

I didn't feel like lying anymore. All I did was nod.

He kicked at the dirt, shaking his head. "So what's your real name?"

I hesitated a second. "It's Patty."

"Okay. Patty."

I said, "I guess it's all over now. Everything."

"I thought it would be. I knew it couldn't last."

I blinked at him. "All along?"

He looked back at me. "Yeah. I knew a girl like you wouldn't stay in San Bavispe."

I tried smiling, but I couldn't keep it up. "If they find out what you did for me, you might go to jail."

"Great."

"I'm sorry."

"So is this it?"

I nodded. "I think so. I think it is."

He thought about it. "Well, don't I even get a good-bye kiss?"

I nodded and walked over to him. It lasted a long time.

He drove me to the nearest town, a small place called Glamis. He pulled into a Texaco station. I started to climb off the bike, but he got off first. He left it running. "You ever ride one of these before?"

"What? No."

"Just like a bicycle."

"Wait a minute."

"This is the throttle," he said, showing me. "Clutch is here. You have to change gears. Like on a ten-speed bike."

"I can't take it."

"Just leave it somewhere for me. I'll report it missing tomorrow or something. Okay? I'll get it back eventually."

"David . . ."

"Here. You gotta wear this." He took off his jacket and made me put it on. "In case you're stupid enough to fall down."

I sighed, then zipped it up. "Right."

Then he put his helmet on me. I thought for a second about Dad showing me how to work the gun. In the end, which would prove more dangerous to me? That gun or this motorcycle? David tightened the helmet strap beneath my chin. He said, "This doesn't fit right, but I guess it'll have to do."

Sitting there on the idling motorcycle, I said, "This isn't right."

"Yeah, but so little is. Besides, you got a driver's license, right?"

"Right. How will you get back to town?"

"I'll hitch it. Don't worry." David looked around and then back at me. "You better get moving. I saw what those creeps looked like."

"Right again," I said.

"What are you going to do about your dad?"

"I don't know."

"Do you have enough money?"

I thought about it. "Yeah. Enough. David . . ."

"Listen, if this isn't a question about the bike I'd rather skip it. Okay?"

"I'm going to miss you."

He swallowed. "I really, really hate goodbyes. Why don't you just leave?"

I was choking up, and I gunned the engine. David yelled at me over the roar. "Be careful! Balance it like a bicycle! Don't go any faster than you have to!"

I took a deep breath. Ready or not.

David said one more thing to me: "Hey!"

I looked over.

"You're beautiful, Patty Whoever-You-Are."

I roared off. Changed gears. Disappeared.

I rode on, watching the horizon. The sand. The clouds. I've always been fascinated by clouds, those shepherds of the sky. They try to make everything right with the world. They don't always succeed, but they try. Good going, guys.

FIFTEEN

It took three hours on the same road to reach the next town. I don't even remember the name. I got some change from the gas station there while the attendant admired the motorcycle. I called the motel in San Bavispe. Just on a chance. When they rang the room, Marshal Rogers answered.

I didn't say anything.

"Patty?"

I hung up. I wasn't worried; there was no way they could have traced the call. I didn't think. I paid for the gas and climbed back on. It took a while for me to start the bike, but eventually I rode off again. Carefully.

I made one important stop between Glamis, California, and Brawley, California. Dad had explained it all well enough, but it still took a while to find. It was after nightfall when I got there — I had to buy a flashlight in town. There was an old railroad shack marked CLEMENTINE.

There was also a body outside, behind it.

I jumped. It wasn't moving; it just lay in the sand.

I was scared. It couldn't be. It wasn't. It just could not be . . .

It wasn't Dad.

It was Skyler. The man with the white hair who had kidnapped me. His eyes were open; there was blood on his chest. He wasn't breathing.

I wasn't doing so well myself.

It had come to this; it had come to this. But who had done it? Dad? Oh, my God . . .

I pushed into the shack. The flashlight beam hit a pile of oily rags and two paint cans. The floor was covered with grit. The shack smelled like turpentine. I stepped further in, moving the light. . . .

A voice said, "Don't move."

I heard a metallic click.

Then, "Okay, look over here."

I did. Lying on the ground, one arm wrapped around his own middle, was Helker. In the other hand he held his gun. Static cackled from his radio, which lay at his feet.

Helker was in bad shape. He licked his lips and waved the gun at me. "You . . ."

I didn't move.

Helker sort of laughed. "That wasn't very nice with the perfume . . . Miss Pelling."

I still didn't move.

222

He nodded, absently. "I need your help."

Just a second. Then I said, "What?"

"I'm hurt. You can see. I need your help."

I shook my head. "After all this? Why should I?"

"Because I'm hurt. Please." He clicked the gun again, tossed it across the shack. It bounced off the far wall and stopped. "There. See? Just help me."

"Where's my dad?"

"I don't know."

"You're lying."

"I'm not. Ask Skyler. He's outside."

"He's dead."

Helker sort of smiled. "Yeah. I know."

I looked at him. "Did you do it?"

Helker just smiled.

I went over and picked up his gun. It was gritty and covered with sand.

"Patty, please . . ."

"I don't owe you anything."

"Please!"

I looked at him and relented a bit. "I'll call somebody at the first pay phone I find. The police. But that's all I'm going to do."

"Please . . ."

"Goodbye."

That's when the radio at Helker's feet cackled. *"Patty? Are you there?"*

Dad was on the other end.

Helker didn't even look surprised. I grabbed the radio and keyed the mike. "Daddy?"

"Go outside, Patty."

"Why?"

"Just go." There was some static.

Taking the radio and gun, I stepped back out into the dark. I had left the motorcycle headlight on, and I carried the flashlight. The radio spoke again. *"Stop. Turn to your left a little. Some more. Stop. Now walk dead ahead, about fifty yards."*

I did. I almost tripped over the suitcase. An old-fashioned tan valise.

I looked around. I couldn't see anything in the dark but the shack and, far behind, Skyler's body. The radio cracked again. Dad. *"Take the bag and get out of here."*

"Where are you?"

Static.

"Dad? Where are you?"

Static.

"Where do we meet?"

Static.

I took the bag.

It wasn't some of the money. It was most of it. I got rid of the gun and the radio and made the phone call I promised Helker, but I don't know if anyone found him in time. It's remarkable how little I care. Dad never showed himself, and I went on to Brawley. I left the motorcycle there and took the Greyhound bus to San Diego.

I had $88,430.

I didn't spend much time in San Diego. It didn't seem to be a good idea. I went straight to the airport. That's where I am now. Nobody around me seems to question, which is just as well. I don't match any of the descriptions, not since I bought the new hair color in Brawley, and besides, I do have luggage.

The reports on radio and television all say that Casper Pelling, pursued by all manner of machine, man, and tracking beast, disappeared into the California desert without a trace. After weeks of searching they'll have to assume he's dead. Nobody could survive out there for long.

But everybody knows better than that, I think.

As for Karen Peterson, I can't go home again. Not as Karen, not as Patty, not even as . . . but there are lots of places I can go.

Before, when things were different, I might have thought it wrong to keep the money, but now I'm not so sure. I will probably keep it. The money will help me blend into the background of wherever I choose to live.

I have an appointment to keep. Just one, a year from now. Other than that, my life is my own. No friends, no family. There will be adjustments, but none as shocking as the one I had to make when I saw Dad — Doug Meely, my real dad — being thrown onto the hood of our car by the FBI guys. That was the hardest. After that, anything comes easy.

One of the few things I bought before heading out to the airport was this notebook. I'll walk away from it when I'm finished, and maybe somebody will turn a page and read some before tossing it into the nearest trash can. Maybe not, but if so do me one favor: If you should pass me on the street and recognize me, from some newspaper photo, please look the other way and say nothing. The damage is already done. And I'm so very tired of running.

PAN HORIZONS

'Easy to pick up, hard to put down'

Toeckey Jones
Skin Deep

Everything was against them. The country, the time . . . and the colour of his skin.

M. E. Kerr
Night Kites

The night of the Springsteen concert was a night for revelations . . . and the start of some lessons in love . . .

Judy Blume
Forever

Catherine and Michael's relationship seems to be forever. But will love last when they are separated?

Bruce Brooks
The Moves Make the Man

Nothing fazes Jerome Fox, not even crossing the road to become the first black student at Wilmington School. But he can't make out Bix Rivers – the sharpest white guy he has ever seen.

Patricia Windsor
The Sandman's Eyes

Accused of a murder he did not commit, Michael must find the real killer for the sake of his sanity.

Richard Peck
Are You In The House Alone?

In spite of the violence she was still alone – victim of a crime that punished the innocent.

Harry Mazer
I Love You, Stupid!

Burning ambition is one thing. Acting out everyone else's lead role is another story altogether . . .

Norma Klein
Beginner's Love

Joel and Leda happily shared so many first times together. But when things go wrong Leda is on her own.

Lois Duncan
The Eyes of Karen Connors

She can see things that no one else can see. She *knows* things she can't possibly know. Where is her power coming from?

Barbara Wersba
Fat – A Love Story

Rita has this problem with men, slimming and cheesecakes – cue romance, Arnold and a new image.

M. E. Kerr
If I Love You, Am I Trapped Forever?

Alan Bennett is cool – or so he thinks. And he just can't understand it when someone else gets all the attention.

Paula Fox
The Moonlight Man

Catherine's quiet and peaceful life is exposed to the mysterious influence of the Moonlight Man.

Merrill Joan Gerber
I'm Kissing as Fast As I Can

Sid's father is all for encouraging his son's love life, but Sid is looking for true love.

Lois Duncan
Stranger With My Face

Was she going crazy? Or was something really horribly sinister casting a shadow across her life?

M. E. Kerr
Is That You, Miss Blue?

Flanders Brown reckoned she was pretty unconventional. But she was no match for the teacher with a direct line through to Jesus.

Virginia Hamilton
A Little Love

The car wasn't up to much. But they had the rest of their lives to make the journey of discovery.

M. E. Kerr
The Son of Someone Famous

Adam needed a friend, but Brenda needed a boyfriend. Together they came up with the perfect solution.

Rosemary Wells
The Man in the Woods

Helen knows somebody's watching her, and it's a nightmare she can't escape.

Merrill Joan Gerber
Also Known as Sadzia! The Belly Dancer

Sandy's fed up with her mother's comments about her size, so she agrees to exercise: with one very strange condition!

Norma Klein
Breaking Up

Now she's back with her father, and her mother's fallen in love with another woman, Alison isn't sure about anything, except her feelings for Ethan.

Barbara Wersba
Crazy Vanilla

Tyler's entry for the vanilla ice-cream naming contest is a bit like him – creative and vague. It takes Mitzi to show him a few of life's other essential ingredients.

Norma Klein
It's OK If You Don't Love Me

Jenny had seen it all, knew it all, and tried everything once. Yet, when it came to the crunch she was the most vulnerable person she knew.

Rosemary Wells
When No One Was Looking

Winning was an obsession. But was it worth someone's life?

Sandra Scoppettone
Happy Endings Are All Alike

Jaret and Peggy choose love, but a disturbed teenager – rejected by Jaret – brings menace to the two girls' lives . . .

Barbara Wersba
Tunes for a Small Harmonica

Enter J. F. McAllister – poor little rich kid and rebel in search of a cause. Exit – one psychoanalyst and a terrified poetry teacher!

C. S. Adler
Binding Ties

Anne's life is dominated by her mother and grandmother, and a passionate affair with Kyle offers the chance of escape – but for how long?

Norma Klein
Going Backwards

He'd waited all this time for a chance to grow up. Now everyone around him was growing old . . .

Lois Duncan
I Know What You Did Last Summer

Somebody know what really happened that night . . . and they'll go to any lengths to get revenge.

Richard Peck
Remembering the Good Times

Calling each other best friends was one thing. But how well did they really know each other?

Richard Peck
Close Enough to Touch

It seemed like a bad dream – as if Dory was really alive and he was the one who was dead. Margaret can help him sort it out, but she won't take self-pity for an answer.

Norma Klein
Angel Face

As the only one still left at home, guess who ended up looking after everything?

Aidan Chambers
Dance On My Grave

From beginning to end it was a dangerous dream which lasted seven weeks. Exactly 49 days. Now the court is demanding some kind of explanation. . . .

John MacLean
Mac

Remembering *that* face drives Mac into a savage fury. He *knows* who's behind his nightmare. And holding it back is driving him crazy.

Jean Thesman
The Last April Dancers

In the darkness magic and madness lie, but first love is a moment of enchantment and dancing in the moonlight.

All Pan books are available at your local bookshop or newsagent, or can be ordered direct from the publisher. Indicate the number of copies required and fill in the form below.

Send to: **CS Department, Pan Books Ltd., P.O. Box 40, Basingstoke, Hants.   RG21 2YT.**

or phone: 0256 469551 (Ansaphone), quoting title, author and Credit Card number.

Please enclose a remittance* to the value of the cover price plus: 60p for the first book plus 30p per copy for each additional book ordered to a maximum charge of £2.40 to cover postage and packing.

*Payment may be made in sterling by UK personal cheque, postal order, sterling draft or international money order, made payable to Pan Books Ltd.

Alternatively by Barclaycard/Access:

Card No.

Signature:

Applicable only in the UK and Republic of Ireland.

While every effort is made to keep prices low, it is sometimes necessary to increase prices at short notice. Pan Books reserve the right to show on covers and charge new retail prices which may differ from those advertised in the text or elsewhere.

NAME AND ADDRESS IN BLOCK LETTERS PLEASE:

....

Name ⎯⎯⎯⎯⎯⎯⎯⎯⎯⎯⎯⎯⎯⎯⎯⎯⎯⎯⎯⎯⎯⎯⎯⎯

Address ⎯⎯⎯⎯⎯⎯⎯⎯⎯⎯⎯⎯⎯⎯⎯⎯⎯⎯⎯⎯⎯

⎯⎯⎯⎯⎯⎯⎯⎯⎯⎯⎯⎯⎯⎯⎯⎯⎯⎯⎯⎯⎯⎯⎯⎯⎯

⎯⎯⎯⎯⎯⎯⎯⎯⎯⎯⎯⎯⎯⎯⎯⎯⎯⎯⎯⎯⎯⎯⎯⎯⎯

3/87